Dark Side

Dark Side

CC Brown

To order additional copies of this book, contact:
Xlibris Corporation
1-888-795-4274
www.Xlibris.com
Orders@Xlibris.com
76030

Dedication

To our family and friends who encouraged us to get our thoughts down on paper. Although they did not understand our obsession with vampires, they never doubted our ability as writers. To Lori Dodson, Connie Dean, and Jean Reynolds, thanks for the memories. We would like to also express our gratitude to Bob Senninger for convincing us that we really could write a fiction book.

Prologue

The armored warrior hacked and slashed his way to the cathedral of Constantinople. He crawled through the rammed hole in the wall and drove back the robed defenders on the other side. A handful of Crusaders followed him. For three days, the knights murdered, raped, looted, and destroyed on a level that even the ancient Roman army would have found deplorable.

While the other knights and men-at-arms went on a drunken rampage, the warrior and his band set to work like hardened criminals, sacking the fallen city. Searching for religious relics and stealing all they could lay their hands on, the thieves brutally and methodically desecrated the city's most holy sanctuaries.

Approaching the altar of the great cathedral, he indiscriminately grabbed anything gold. His plunder stopped as he beheld the faded script of the open scroll. It was the last thing added to his loot before he fled.

The warrior disappeared and with him all traces of the treasures. Hidden . . . Forgotten . . . Centuries passed, the dark secrets of the scroll were lost to the world until . . .

Chapter 1

The Watcher's instructions had been clear. Attend the auction, secure the artifact, and return it to the Council.

K oleen spent most of her weekends at estate sales held around the Ozarks, picking up collectibles for her antique store. Rummaging through tables full of old pottery, figurines, silver, and linens always revealed lots of vintage items. She had recently scooped up several great bargains including a turn-of-the-century ornate glass whale oil lamp. On rare occasions, she came across unique items that appealed only to a select group of treasure hunters: artifacts that were believed to be associated with paranormal events. Her most recent acquisition had been an absolutely stunning hand-carved antique oak box. Even though the bidding was fast and furious, Koleen had stolen the wooden box for $170.

Koleen dumped her purse, auction bargains, and plastic grocery bag on the L-shaped granite kitchen counter. She began putting away the few necessities she had picked up on the way home from the late-afternoon sale.

"Hey, Buck," she said to the golden lab. Lonely, she adopted the five-year-old dog from the no-kill shelter after the disappearance of her husband. Blissfully wagging his tail, he waited expectantly.

While digging in one of the plastic grocery bags, Koleen teased, "Look what I've got for you." She offered the dog his favorite treat—a large rawhide bone. Content, Buck plopped down by the kitchen table with his prize and chewed.

Koleen made quick work of putting away the groceries. As she passed the kitchen window on the way to the refrigerator, she was distracted. A full moon was rising. The local news anchor had called it a "wolf moon," a name, he said, that dated back to Native American culture. They believed that packs of hungry wolves howled at the full moon.

Opening the door to get a beer, she noticed the two uncorked champagne bottles left over from New Year's Eve. *Had it really been six months since Riley's vanishing act?*

Somehow, she had missed all the warning signs. In the middle of the holiday celebration and a house full of guests, Riley's cell phone rang. After a few quick, frantic whispers, he snapped it shut, avoiding Koleen's questioning look. Shoving the phone in a pocket, he made his apologies, grabbed the black overcoat hanging by the door, and rushed out. "Emergency . . . company business . . . no time for explanations."

Anger boiling, she followed to the garage, demanding to know where he was going. The asshole stood, both hands pressed to the roof of his new silver Jag—Riley's Christmas present to Riley. He turned, grim-faced, and declared in a weary voice, "I'm not happy. You're just not . . . corporate wife material. I want . . . out." Too stunned to speak, Koleen watched him back and speed off. She struggled to control the raging inferno of anger that threatened to consume her. Muscles tensed, fists clenched, she gave in. No one heard her cry out.

In the house, the noisy celebration continued without Koleen and Riley. At the stroke of midnight, champagne corks popped, and party horns sounded. Shouts of "Happy New Year" could be heard over the melody of "Auld Lang Syne."

The following afternoon, a county deputy phoned. He reported that Riley's abandoned and vandalized Jag had been discovered on a farm road near their home. Months passed, and Riley's whereabouts remained a mystery.

She grabbed a beer and hugged Buck, who abandoned his bone to nuzzle her hand. Dogs were a great comfort; they loved you unconditionally.

Sitting at the kitchen table, nursing the beer, Koleen reached for the wooden box she had placed on the counter. She lifted the lid and peered inside. It was empty. She closed the lid and turned it over to inspect the bottom. As she rubbed her hand across the smooth surface, she paused on what felt like a flaw. *Damn,* she thought. *There goes my profit.* Koleen tried to determine how this discovery might affect the resale value. Running her fingers over the small blemish again, she was startled when a hidden drawer sprung open, hitting and spilling her brew on the table. Mopping up the mess, it dawned on Koleen that she had a rare treasure on her hands. What at first had appeared to be an ordinary wooden box was what antique dealers called a "book safe." Better yet, wedged inside the interior of the secret tray, lay a black leather-bound manuscript. The deeply textured cover was worn with age and use.

Buck growled, backed away, and stood barking. Laying the book on the table, she moved to comfort him. Buck sat on his haunches, directing low, uneasy growls towards it.

Spooked by the dog's behavior, Koleen drained what was left of her drink. She was still unnerved; her hand shook slightly as she threw the empty bottle in the trash. Returning her attention to the book, she picked it up and tried to open the latch on the front. It wouldn't budge. Noticing a key in the bottom of the tray, she placed it in the latch and gave it a turn. With a soft click, the pages fell open.

Quickly scanning several of the worn pages, Koleen became immersed in the intricate, detailed characters and pagan symbols. The document was written in an unfamiliar ancient script. Deep in thought she took the manuscript to her office. Within minutes, she was cross-legged on the floor surrounded by volumes of opened reference books.

Time stood still as she called on her expertise as a linguist of dead languages to decipher the scribbled characters and drawings. Engrossed in her search for answers, the code of the mysterious script began to unravel. The key pieces to the puzzle fell into place as the clock over her desk struck the midnight hour. The language consisted of about 600 symbols; each represented a syllable or word fragment. The syllables could be used as single words or combined with others, and they often had multiple meanings. She read no further when she stumbled upon and decoded the chilling prophecy . . .

Once deemed sacred by man, the night calls to the thirst . . . those who possess the courage, will find in the darkness what eluded them in the light . . . life beyond death . . . immortality.

Straightening her shoulders, Koleen reminded herself to take in air. The yellowed parchment revealed a dark secret. The wooden box held the sacred text of the world of the undead. It was the fabled . . . long-lost . . . much-sought. . . Vampire Bible. Many scholars believed it was destroyed when the Crusaders of Western Europe invaded and conquered the Christian city of Constantinople, capital of the Byzantine Empire.

Shaken by her discovery, Koleen closed and locked the book, threaded the key on the chain hanging around her neck, and placed the Bible back in the tray. Shutting the secret compartment and ignoring uneasiness, a hint of a smile tugged at the edge of her lips. The $170 investment was about to make her a millionaire.

Koleen was a confirmed skeptic when it came to the supernatural world, but selling relics believed to be connected in some way to paranormal phenomena did pay the rent and put food on the table. She was successful at what she did because she had developed a solid business philosophy. "There's a sucker born everyday. All you have to do is bait the hook and wait." With this attitude driving her and a few days of planning, she devised a brilliant scheme for unloading the book . . . World Wide Web.

She knew from experience, those things that were perceived as forbidden and secretive held an unexplainable allure for some people. The Vampire Bible was thought by many to be a passport into the dark world of the undead. Vampire myths went back thousands of years and occurred in almost every culture around the world. Even after centuries of study, there still wasn't a scholarly consensus as to the origin of vampirism or the name of the first vampire. The sacred book of the undead was believed to hold the secret. If the legend was to be believed, it traced the lineage of the vampires back to their beginning.

The legend was fascinating, but what Koleen found most intriguing was the thousands of bids she had gotten when her assistant put the book safe and Vampire Bible up for sale on eBay. Using the legend as bait, she hooked a whopper! The highest bidder was from an individual in San Antonio, Texas. Not trusting the transaction to a middle man, Koleen planned to deliver the artifact in person.

That damn scrawny freckled-faced redhead. Her aggressive bidding style had totally distracted him. She definitely relished every moment of the competition. Caught up in her antics, he was startled when the auctioneer shouted, "Sold to number twenty-four!"

Entering the mind of the cashier at the estate sale had been a breeze. Koleen O'Brien lived at 302 Washem Hollow Road in the town of Rescue. But his efforts to get into to the redhead's thoughts and take control had failed miserably. Most mortals were easy to manipulate. Slip in, plant a thought, and BAM, they were ripe for the pickin'. Maybe he was losing his touch. Well, it was obvious; he wasn't going to get the artifact by planting suggestions in her head.

Getting the book had now become a problem for vampires adhered to the "Vampire Code." They had to obey it like humans were required to obey mortal laws. No, he couldn't attack her in public, attracting unwanted attention to retrieve the book nor could he enter Koleen's home without being invited and steal it from her. Abide by the code, or break it and face the consequences. Punishment in his world wasn't a mere slap on the wrist or hours of community service—it was annihilation by staking.

The Council had instructed him to set up surveillance and monitor her every move. He would bide his time. She would slip up, and he would be there when she did.

Chapter 2

The Watcher's patience soon paid off. A small late model Nissan pulled up to the curb. Several moments passed as he studied each of the six women piling out. It was time to take control of the situation and the Bible. Once the sacred book was in his possession, he would erase the women's memories and be on his way. He reached out with his power, directing it purposefully. Wrapping his will around them, he cast his dark veil of control. Nothing . . . his thoughts fell discarded around the group of six. Determined he tried again. He hurled a blast of psychic energy at each of them. Nothing, not even a psychic twitch.

Koleen and Dominic sprinted across the parking lot. They headed for the airport terminal, anxious to get the rental, a roomy SUV, and be on their way. Raven strolled to the nearest shaded bench for a smoke. Jaylyn and Mona unloaded the tightly packed luggage from the trunk of Mona's car. They started wheeling the bags to the terminal. Angel, a retired registered nurse, was left alone to rummage through her pharmaceutical bag. She was a walking, talking drugstore, dispensing medication she deemed necessary. Her brown hair, attractively streaked with silver, was ruffled by the slight breeze as she gingerly opened the black satchel. "Ibuprofen, check. Antacid tablets, check. Sharpened, wooden stakes, **double check**." She had adopted the motto "Be prepared for anything, even the unknown" since her husband's untimely passing.

Angel had met the others at a bereavement counseling program recommended by her therapist after the death of George, her husband. Finding it hard to open up in a large group setting, the six had started meeting after the weekly sessions at a nearby bar. A comment made by one of the women over drinks resonated with the group. "Sometimes, there is only one good solution for a bad marriage." After that night, the confidences that couldn't be shared in a bright, airy conference room with twenty other grieving widows were easily disclosed in the dimly lit atmosphere of the bar. They realized that their dark secrets forged a sinister bond that could never be broken. No one remembered exactly how they had settled on the name "Black Widow Society," but they all agreed it was appropriate, considering the female of the black widow spider species commonly ate the male after mating.

Anxious to get on the road, Raven watched the airport traffic. Cars pulled in and out, people rushed to catch their flights. Scanning the parking lot, violent shivers rocked her. *Had someone or something just stepped over my grave?* she wondered. Raven knew not to ignore her premonitions; they were a warning.

Koleen carried the "trip folder," which she had so diligently organized over the past months. Reservations, sightseeing schedule, trip budget, and road maps were all neatly arranged inside the folder. Everything had been checked and rechecked including the confirmation of the vehicle and motel reservations.

Dominic and Koleen entered the airport and located the car rental booth. As she stepped up to the counter, Koleen pushed up her glasses and greeted the clerk manning the desk. The group had used this company on several occasions and found it to be a pleasant experience with no glitches. The rates were fair, and the service had been flawless.

Opening the trip folder, Koleen proceeded to give the woman all the relevant information. The clerk reviewed and confirmed the reservation on her computer. The printout of the rental terms and agreement were slid to Koleen for a signature.

Dominic, a combination of sultry sophistication and sexiness, watched as Koleen scanned the paper and paused on the price. Dominic stood on tiptoes and peeked over her shoulder. The price was not the same as quoted; in fact, it had doubled. Koleen's green eyes flashed red!

The wary clerk perceived a confrontation and stepped back. Dominic knew that look all too well. *Oh, boy*, Dominic thought as she gave Koleen room for what was to follow. *The agreement over the terms of the car rental reservation was just about to get ugly.* It had been duly noted by everyone in the group that the disappearance of Koleen's husband had left her a bit unhinged. Recently, she had been exhibiting some unusual tendencies, one of which was zero tolerance for what she saw as incompetency.

"What the hell is going on? Is the manager here?" Koleen began her first line of questioning.

The elderly woman stood her ground and insisted that there was no error. "The computer doesn't lie," she smirked.

"Wrong answer, bitch!" Koleen yelled. She suddenly reached over the counter and hooked "Ms. Know-It All" by the collar of her cheap shirt.

Dominic grabbed Koleen's arm. "You promised your anger management coach that you would refrain from using profanity when you get in one of your rages."

The terrified employee snatched up the phone and called manager Bob immediately after Koleen loosened her grip. Bob detected the severity of the situation and directed the clerk to fix and print a new agreement.

"This is more like it." Seeing that things were back on track, the clerk then turned to the board behind the desk and reached for the keys. Her hand hesitated and started to tremble. A look of total disbelief swept over her face. The keys were missing. Frantically, Granny clicked on the computer screen.

In a quivering voice, she said, "I do not know how this happened, but the SUV was rented yesterday. All we have available is a compact car."

It was Koleen's turn to grab Dominic's arm. Koleen was crazy. But when provoked, Dominic was quick to even the score with physical violence. The Black Widows considered Dominic's hands lethal weapons since she had completed her online course in tae kwon do. After her husband had been mugged and murdered in an alley, she vowed that she would never be defenseless.

"Your wrinkled, old neck is mine now!" Dominic screamed as her caramel-colored ponytail whipped around her head.

Koleen managed to drag Dominic to the side, explaining that they didn't need a murder rap on their hands. "Remember, some of us are still considered 'persons of interest' in ongoing investigations."

Dominic simmered as the pathetic worker snatched the cordless phone and hit speed dial.

The rest of the gang, tired of waiting, had filed into the airport, adding to the chaos. By this time, people in the bag check line noticed the commotion. Someone, fearing for the clerk's safety, had alerted airport security. Hand on gun, the guard slowly approached the pandemonium. The assistant held up her hand, signaling that everything was under control. "Bob is sending a van!" Silence blanketed the airport waiting area.

In total agreement, the ladies shrugged. "All right, we'll wait outside and inspect it when it gets here." Koleen snatched up the paperwork and stomped out.

"Damn straight we will!" Dominic cursed. The gang strutted behind the two as they headed for the parking lot.

Koleen glanced as a suspicious man dodged to the side of the entrance as they were leaving. *How odd*, she thought. *It was almost like he didn't want to be seen.* Even though she had only gotten a glimpse of his face hidden beneath dark glasses, Koleen thought she had seen him somewhere before.

He hated to admit it, but he was responsible for what had just transpired inside the airport terminal. Using his power of suggestion, he had easily convinced the car rental clerk to give him the silver SUV with tinted windows on her reserved list. Boy, what a mistake. His actions had drawn unnecessary attention. But hell, if he was required to chase these clearly deranged women all over the southwest, then he was going to do it in luxury. He was not traveling in a midsized economy car. That just wasn't going to happen!

A smile crossed the Watcher's face as he picked up the unintentionally discarded paper and read. Here was the opening he had been waiting for.

Chapter 3

The Watcher followed at a safe distance. No need to hurry; he knew their destination, the Hotel Valencia. The paper dropped by the redhead contained the information he needed.

Inside the red van, organized chaos reigned. Everyone was talking at once about the van rental ordeal. Koleen kept whining, "We are behind schedule." The women knew that if she did not keep to the trip schedule, they would never hear the end of it. She would bellyache all the way to San Antonio. Dominic was ranting about how she could have taken the old lady with her "Eye of the Tiger" move while demonstrating the hand motions to Angel, who was trying to get everyone to take a Valium to steady their nerves.

While munching on a chocolate donut, Mona leaned over the backseat, giving Jaylyn a graphic and lurid description of what she would have enjoyed doing to the cute airport guard. Mona never worried about her weight. At any given point in time, one or more of the women were dieting. Not Mona.

She ate and drank whatever took her fancy without a second thought to calories or carbohydrates. Her philosophy: "Why bother? Men adored full-figured women because they liked having something soft to hang on to while in the saddle. It would be cruel to deny men something that gave them such obvious pleasure." Her last lover fondly described her as a late model, hard body with running boards.

At twenty-five, Jaylyn, the youngest of the group, sat quietly. Blond hair formed a curtain around her face as she wrote in her journal. A lab technician, she performed E. Coli and salmonella tests on poultry products. Sadly, her husband had suffered an agonizing illness due to food poisoning. Blood tests detected high levels of salmonella bacteria in his system, which had led to his death. It was later linked to the nationwide recall of contaminated peanut butter. How ironic!

Jaylyn found her work interesting, but it didn't tap what she called her "creative juices." Her real talent lay in turning words and ideas into rhyming verses. The group was pleasantly surprised that she had taken on the task of documenting their trips as a series of poems. Jaylyn had them rollin' in the aisles when she shared the hilarious interpretations at their annual Christmas party.

Paranoid, Raven's eyes darted from the rearview mirror to the side mirror. She wondered, *Were they being followed? Time to find out.* Being an avid NASCAR fan, Raven knew exactly what to do. Punching the accelerator and switching lanes, the van shot past a tour bus and motor home, towing a jeep. The Hummer followed. Her heart hammered, and the adrenaline pumped, giving her a rush. After passing a string of cars trapped between an eighteen-wheeler crawling up the incline, she checked again. The black Hummer was nowhere in sight.

Pressing the pedal to the metal, the needle of the speedometer climbed past eighty. Everyone's attention was quickly diverted from their individual pursuits when they noticed Raven. Her hand reached for a cigarette.

"Who the hell do you think you are, Dale Earnhardt Jr.?" Mona yelled.

"Yeah, this is a van not a racecar!" Dominic added.

Raven reduced her speed. Rattled, she lit the cigarette to calm her nerves. Changing the subject, she snapped, "Where's my GPS?" The black-haired, forty-eight-year-old, Cherokee beauty was hyperventilating. "You damn well know that I can't drive without a GPS!" In fact, Raven had been a first-rate school bus driver for many years; but whenever she left the state, reality set in, and a GPS was a necessity!

As the self-designated driver, Raven claimed she had earned the right. "Anyone who can turn their back on sixty screaming kids and show no fear is more than capable of playing chauffeur for this group. Besides," she pointed out, "it's virtually impossible to get me lost because of my genes. I inherited my excellent sense of direction from my Cherokee ancestors."

The women had learned that it was best not to question Raven's abilities as a driver. She had been behind the wheel the fateful night of the accident that left her a widow. Although the sisterhood promised impenetrable secrecy, none of the group wanted to fall victim to the retelling of Raven's sad tale. The other women lived with Raven's eccentricities by humoring her. Besides, everyone knew she had a few loose screws. As her friends, they recognized having a GPS didn't really matter. It had been dually noted that on several occasions, the new innovation and Raven's "excellent sense of direction" had gotten them lost.

"Here, try breathing into this," Koleen insisted as she stuffed the paper bag over Raven's nose and mouth.

"Get that stupid bag out of my face!" Raven exploded.

Adding her two cents' worth, Dominic explained, "I read on *medicaldoctor.com* that when some people are frightened, they breathe rapidly and deeply even though they don't need the extra oxygen. This causes them to breathe out a large amount of carbon dioxide, and . . ."

"Quit flappin' your jaws, I'm trying to drive." Raven barreled down the interstate, keeping one eye on her mirrors.

Koleen brightened when she remembered the maps. "Well, I did bring these just in case; and look; I have the route marked in red!"

As Koleen discussed the maps with Raven, Dominic leaned over to Mona and whispered, "Remember our last trip? We drove up and down the same freeway for hours before we could talk Raven into pulling over and asking for directions. Big help the maps were then!"

Mona whispered back, "Wasn't it hilarious that we took that photo of our car parked under the gigantic billboard that read 'Lost' while waiting for her?"

Settling into the monotonous stream of traffic, Raven focused on the road ahead. She turned the radio on and tuned the others out. In the back of her mind, she sensed "trouble" not far behind.

He was a great warrior, unmatched in hand-to-hand combat, victorious in battle. It was apparent he was going to have to change his tactics to battle these women.

Chapter 4

He watched the cat-and-mouse game between the van and the Hummer. He would need all his energy if his suspicions were confirmed. Reaching in the Styrofoam cooler, he retrieved his favorite beverage—a cold synthetic bottle of blood, type AB-.

D ominic cleared her throat and declared in a firm voice, "Since I won the last fantasy-reality vacation game, I had the honor of choosing the theme for this game. We're going to be vampire hunters. We're even going to attend a vampire convention!"

"This is beginning to look like a setup to me. Does this have anything to do with that damn Vampire Bible Koleen is delivering to the Texas oilman?" Mona demanded, seething with righteous indignation.

Sticking her tongue out at Mona, Koleen explained, "No and yes. It's really just a coincidence. I bought the artifact at an auction. I thought I could . . . ," she paused, choosing her words carefully, "let's say, 'Kill two birds with one stone.' Deliver the artifact and still have time to enjoy all San Antonio has to offer. So don't get your panties in a wad. Since when have you been opposed to meeting a good-looking, wealthy man?"

"I've done quite a bit of research on the topic of vampires this past year." Dominic, a researcher for an erotica, paranormal, romance writer, spent her days and often nights glued to the computer. Her Internet searches took her to some disturbing and often chilling sites. Therefore, she was always full of useless information that, to the chagrin of her friends, she took great pleasure in sharing. "It's true; vampires are creatures of the night—living in the shadows and feeding in the darkness off humans. But it is just a myth that they can't endure sunlight. So remember; if you run into a vampire on our trip, don't be surprised if they don't explode when sunlight hits them."

"As Rod Sterling would say, you are now entering the Twilight Zone," mocked Mona in deep voice.

"Do-do-do-do," hummed Angel and Jaylyn in unison.

"Hell, Dominic told me she would run home every day after school to watch reruns of some supernatural gothic soap opera filled with vampires, zombies, and werewolves," Koleen poked fun at her friend.

Everyone started laughing but Dominic.

"Hey guys, I think she believes this crap!" Raven proclaimed contemptuously.

"Go ahead, laugh it up, but this is my game. So you had better learn and stick to the rules." Ignoring the teasing, Dominic opened the large brown paper sack at her feet and started handing out small black gift bags containing everything each woman would need for the game. "To play the role of vampire slayers, we need to look authentic. So, I have selected a few tools of the trade for each of us to carry." She pulled a gold crucifix from her black bag and continued, "The cross has the ability to combat evil. It will only have power over evil if you believe in its power. If you don't believe, then the crucifix will be useless."

Next, she displayed a small vial. "This contains baby tears; they're more potent than holy water. When cast upon a vampire, it burns like acid, totally disintegrating them." Dominic smiled and pulled out another small container. "This is my own creation. I call it "Estee de Garlic" perfume. Spray it on your neck before you go to sleep. Its power might save your life!"

Without hesitation, Mona blurted out, "Well, you're out of your flippin' mind if you think I'm spraying that on my neck! I hope you brought some freakin' stakes. That's the only way I'm vampire hunting."

With a raised eyebrow, Dominic turned to Angel, "Did you remember the stakes?"

"Yeah, got 'em. Here they are." She winked. "Call me old-fashioned, but I dipped them in holy water."

Dominic demonstrated how to use one of the wooden daggers. "You can either stab them with the stake or drive it in with a hammer. Remember, the stake must penetrate the vampire's heart to destroy it."

"Hell, if that doesn't work, try one of these," interrupted Mona, opening her own bag of goodies. She tossed pink-colored gag gifts to the others. As they recognized what they had a hold of, squeals erupted. Hee-hawing at their reactions, she teased, "A rubber dick is better than a stake any day."

"Okay, okay, settle down, girls and put your sex toys away," Dominic scolded. "Now, to the scoring of the game." Dominic pulled a scorecard from her bag and signaled for everyone to do the same. "You earn points for each of the items listed on the scorecard including staking a vampire. You automatically lose the game if a vampire bites your neck and sucks your blood."

"Well," Mona said, "if a vampire bites your neck, you will be more than a loser. You'll be dead!"

Ignoring the snickers, Dominic finished, "One last thing, the person with the most points at the end of trip will be declared the winner. That lucky person will get to choose the next vacation theme."

Head pounding, Raven yelled to Angel, "Hey, you got any good drugs back there in that little black satchel of yours? Either Dominic's crap about vampires or me practicing her mind control techniques has given me a headache." In the back of her mind, she knew it wasn't the mind control. She didn't believe in it, and she certainly hadn't been wasting her time practicing it.

As Angel passed the pills to the front, Koleen whispered a warning, "I wouldn't take that if I were you. You could be dead by morning. Remember, her husband supposedly died from an overdose of generic pain killer."

The pain was so excruciating. Raven believed she was either having an aneurysm, or as much as she hated to admit it, an uninvited guest was clawing at her brain. *Maybe I should have practiced that mind-control, mumbo-jumbo garbage after all.* Ignoring Koleen's warning, she popped the pills and caught a glimpse of the Hummer.

The Watcher had been gently pushing around the edges of each woman's mind all afternoon. And finally, he had found a crack in one of their defenses. The woman called Raven had let down her guard to focus on driving. This left her vulnerable to his persistent probing. What he had learned, he didn't like.

The Watcher swore under his breath. These women were posing as modern-day, vampire slayers. He knew the persecution of vampires came in waves, but he had thought the craze had finally died out. Life had been pretty tense for his people during the fifteenth and sixteenth centuries. In Europe, hundreds of thousands of vampires and witches had been rounded up and burned at the stake during the ignorance of the Inquisition. Then, the vampire scare went into decline before becoming a big issue again and peaking in the late 1800s with the damn publication of the highly publicized Bram Stoker book. Dracula's eating habits had made the disgusting practice of vampire slaying an honorable profession yet again. The invention of synthetic blood at the beginning of the twentieth century had eliminated mortals as part of the vampire food chain.

These women were nothing more than occult junkies playing some kind of crazy game. And yet the Watcher knew it was a dangerous masquerade that could end in a battle for their very lives.

Chapter 5

The Watcher let down his guard. What kind of trouble could the women possibly get into driving down the interstate?

Raven accelerated eating up the miles toward their destination. The gang had settled into a more relaxed atmosphere while traveling through Oklahoma. However, the trip got a bit more interesting after crossing the Texas line.

Sure enough, the black Hummer was in the passing lane, maintaining a constant speed with their van. "They're looking our way!" Koleen announced. "We've definitely sparked their interest. Six of them, six of us. How convenient."

Almost afraid to take a breath, Raven glanced to her left. "Trouble" had found them.

"Damn, that one looks like an 'Action Hero' straight out of some adventure movie." They all agreed he was a stud muffin with his sexy short blond faux hawk hair cut and a smile to die for. "He's going on my Real Man Calendar!" Mona proclaimed. As an amateur photographer, Mona had some regional success with a promotional calendar she had created for a local businessman. She had talked the group into modeling for the calendar one snowy January when they had all spent the day drinking margaritas and taking shots of Jose Cuervo. No one was exactly sure how they wound up naked in the woods, bent over in the snow with their bare bottoms raised to the heavens. And no one was more shocked than the women when they saw the calendar with their butts on display at the local bar. Mona had so aptly named it "Butts in the Snow." The calendar was an instant success. Everyone in town was still trying to figure out whose butts were featured on the cover. The real kicker was the black widow spider tattooed on the upper right portion of each butt cheek.

"So, how are you going to get the studs to pose for your calendar? They haven't been plied with liquor like we were," Jaylyn asked, still resentful of how the group had been tricked into posing for that stupid butt calendar.

Ignoring Jaylyn, Mona propped her feet up on the back of Raven's seat and began polishing her toenails. "I'll think of something," Mona replied.

Dominic couldn't pass up the opportunity to torment Mona while she had her hands occupied, brush in one hand, polish in the other. Dominic slipped the rubber, dick gag gift on her middle finger and started making obscene gestures. "Oh, finger puppet, oh, finger puppet," she teased as she rubbed the pink tip up and down Mona's neck.

"Get that damn thing off me!" Mona shrieked as she brushed it aside with her hand. "I'm going to tell you where you can put that in a minute."

Dominic kept tormenting Mona, and then it happened. The dick slipped from her hands, hit the nail polish, and knocked it to the floor between Mona's legs.

"Shit, oh shit. You made me drop it!"

"Remember, this is a rental," scowled Koleen. "Find the bottle and clean up the mess!"

"Oh, I'll get it," Dominic volunteered as she rose and bent over Mona's lap, digging on the floor, trying to get the bottle before the polish got everywhere. As she wiggled around to locate the nail polish, her denim mini skirt slid to her waist, giving the world a view of her new hot pink thong.

The "Honeys" in the Hummer didn't get any further than the window with Dominic's well-rounded ass pressed up against the glass. The look on their faces was priceless! The hunks mistakenly thought they had a front-row seat to an X-rated lesbian sex show.

Mona's eyes twinkled with mischief and humor. "Here's a chance for us to see how far these boys want to take things!" Placing one hand on Dominic's back, she sucked in a ragged breath. "Oh, yeah, right there," she encouraged. The babes were glued to her performance as she raked a hand through her long auburn hair. Mona's body convulsed, and she breathed a sigh, "Mmm-hmm."

"What a drama queen," Jaylyn declared with a wicked chuckle, turning to Angel. They could plainly view Mona's impromptu theatrics. What made the stage show so deliciously depraved was the fact that Dominic was totally unaware of the part she was playing in the pornographic performance.

The hunks had rolled down their windows to get the full effect. Mona focused on the "Action Hero" look-alike. Making eye contact, she suggestively placed two fingers in her mouth and moved them in and out, slowly sucking them. As she arched her back, the white T-shirt strained against her voluptuous breasts.

"Action Hero" watched as a blush of color rose in her cheeks. She didn't look away from his stare. He noticed a sudden difference in her breathing. It was shallow then fast; excitement coursed through him. Predatory instincts erupted like a long dormant volcano. He wanted to quench his thirst. Thoughts of the danger were overridden by his all-consuming need to possess her.

Mona loved to use her sexuality to tease. It was a powerful weapon in the art of seduction, allowing her to find out where the breaking point was in a man. This information was used to control them. She had often used it to reduce normal, intelligent guys to slobbering idiots.

Sensing Dominic was about to give up the search for the elusive polish, Mona urged her on while playacting for her audience in the Hummer. "Don't stop now, Baby. You almost have it."

Losing control, the Hummer began swerving. The driver eventually managed to pull the beast to the shoulder and stop before overturning.

Raven was relieved to see the Hummer safely pulled off the road. *Who the hell do they think they are?* Raven sped up until the Hummer was a tiny speck in the mirror. *Screw them!* she thought.

Dominic straightened, sat down, and held up the nail polish. "Damn, Mona, I almost smothered down there. You were absolutely no help at all."

With a resigned sigh, Raven asked, "Are you two through playing around back there? We need gas, and Koleen has to pee."

"This is our last stop before we hit San Antonio." Glancing at her watch, she announced, "You only have a few minutes. We're behind schedule, so get in, get out, and don't linger," Koleen warned as the van shot down the exit ramp.

The Watcher was irritated as hell! The women had intentionally gone out of their way to attract the attention of the roving band of misfits he had been warned about. No longer content with being banished to the shadows, the renegades were openly moving among mortals. Only one thing would make them take the risk, the artifact.

The truth about vampirism had been shrouded in myth for so many centuries it was no longer possible to distinguish fact from fiction. The artifact contained the true history. The Elders believed it traced the lineage of the Kindred back to the very first vampire on Earth.

The Council was greatly troubled by the fact that a dangerous attraction for the children of the night had gripped the world, thanks to the success of several recent works of fiction. Popular novelists had drawn unwanted notoriety to the vampire condition. These writers had foolishly glamorized the world of the undead with their best-selling books. It seemed women couldn't get enough of these bad boys of the night. They were portrayed as larger-than-life entities—charismatic, powerful, and mysterious. They had defeated death and were rewarded with eternal life. Their superhuman strength, agility, and speed allowed them to easily demolish their enemies.

The legend of the seductive vampire and the alluring mystique of "forbidden love" had ignited an obsession with anything vampire. Teenage girls and even grown-up women loved the vampire tales of blood and lust. They swooned at the idea of a vampire mesmerizing them, capturing their mind, and holding them in a hypnotized state for the sole purpose of snacking on their blood while engaging in wild sex. The Watcher knew from experience; many women found all of this highly erotic. This obsession fueled the desire of many to uncover the truth about the power and existence of vampires.

Wearily, the Watcher rubbed his hand over his thick, dark hair. He knew with certainty that at some point, he would be forced to make contact with these foolish women, and he found this thought most distasteful. "It would be much healthier for mortals if they just kept their damn noses out of vampire business," he thought.

Chapter 6

Ending the call from the Council, the Watcher shoved the cell in his pocket. Big problem . . . Ancient Ones. His connection on the council had informed him of a mole in the organization. They suspected that one of the Elders was leaking vital intel to the rogues. This posed a threat to his mission.

Considered a serious menace by the Council, these rogues were the most dangerous and powerful of all vampires. Their existence could be traced back to the Crusades. Surviving for centuries, their supernatural powers had developed over time, becoming stronger as they aged. They had gained a tolerance for sunlight and could be out in it for short periods of time without experiencing any ill effects. That explained their ability to move around in broad daylight.

All vampires needed to consume blood to survive and repair damage done to their bodies even the Ancient Ones. The renegades would have to feed soon. Rejecting synthetic blood, they would require human victims. They had found a two-for-one deal in the women: dinner and the trophy book.

The self-service station was alive with customers filling up their vehicles and paying inside. Raven pulled up and parked at one of the empty pumps. She guessed low gas prices had attracted budget-conscious travelers because most of the cars and trucks fueling had out-of-state plates.

Raven, dogged by Dominic, stepped around the side of the van, read the fueling instructions, punched the "pay inside" button, and started filling the tank. Money in hand, Jaylyn and Angel pushed through the store doors and headed to the snack display. Raven followed their progress until her eyes were drawn to the Texas Lottery advertisement. She turned to Dominic. "Hey, I'll finish here. Pick me up a couple of those Texas Mega Millions Lottery tickets. The jackpot is sixty-nine million, and while you're there, get me five of those two-dollar scratch-offs."

Dominic's shoulders slumped; she took off her dark glasses and pinched the bridge of her nose. She placed the glasses on top of her head and attempted a weary smile. Her gaze wandered over the parking lot and then zeroed in on Raven. No sense avoiding the obvious, she decided. "I've been meaning to talk to you about what the Gamblers Anonymous organization calls the *hidden illness*, she began gently.

Confused, Raven looked at Dominic. "What are you talking about?" Then, it dawned on her. "Am I wrong to assume this is more of your Internet bull?"

Dominic waved her hand vaguely and didn't comment for a moment. She chose her words, carefully determined to continue. "Yes, but let me explain. I am concerned about you. You have all the classic symptoms of a compulsive gambler."

"I am not a compulsive gambler. I am a recreational gambler. I do it for fun, and only when I am traveling with you, dumb asses!" Raven fired back.

"Sign number one—compulsive gamblers deny or minimize their problem," pointed out Dominic with a know-it-all grin.

Raven was tempted to slap that look right off Dominic's face. *Dominic is such an idiot*, Raven decided. She did not want or deserve a lecture from Miss Goodie-Two-Shoes. "I am not hurting anyone. Besides, you and the other members of the Black Widow Society are the only ones who know I gamble."

Dominic reached out and patted her friend on the arm. Raven bristled but said nothing, letting Dominic finish her sermon on the evils of gambling.

"Sign number two—problem gamblers go to great lengths to hide their behavior. I have the website address for Gamblers Anonymous. It's a twelve-step recovery program patterned after Alcoholics Anonymous."

Raven stopped pumping gas, closed her eyes, and put her fingers in her ears. She shook her head from side to side while screaming "Blah-blah-blah-blah-blah-blah!" at the top of her lungs.

Dominic reached over and pulled Raven's fingers from her ears. "There is help for this 'impulse-control disorder' you have. When you are ready, I am here to help."

Her now open eyes shot at Dominic. "That's enough!" The icy stare chilled Dominic to her very soul. As she took a step backward, Raven took a step forward, deliberately shoving Dominic. "Don't forget my other problem," warned Raven. "The state of Missouri thinks I am an excellent candidate for vehicular manslaughter. Many of my friends and neighbors think I am a cold-blooded killer. I joined a self-help group called the Black Widow Society. It also has a twelve-step program. At this very moment, I am contemplating falling off the wagon considering the great pleasure it would give me to wring your damn neck!"

Panic lit Dominic's blue eyes. Scared as hell, she backed and turned to the safety of the store. *It might be a good idea to indulge Raven one more time and pick up those tickets,* she thought. As her mother always said, "It is better to run away and live to fight another day." *Indeed, a very wise woman.*

Returning to the van, Koleen and Mona watched the confrontation. They were confident that Raven and Dominic could work out any differences without their help. They were perfectly content to watch the heavy flow of traffic in and out of the station. "Hey, look, the babes need gas too," squealed Koleen. The black Hummer had pulled up at the pump farthest from the van.

Mona snapped up her camera and hit the pavement running. "Here's my chance to get a picture for my Real Man Calendar." She was determined to make a pinup calendar of men who looked like men, not pretty boys.

Koleen watched the scene unfold in front of her. With a flip of her wild, gypsy hair and a wiggle of her curvaceous hips, Mona moved forward, camera clicking. It was well known that she was a "man magnet."

Mr. "Action Hero" stepped from the Hummer, immediately aware of the approaching beauty. He licked his lips and moved to meet her; his long stride relaxed and confident.

Meeting in the middle of the parking lot, his control over her became clear. Mona stood frozen, inviting his warm, welcoming smile. He reached out and stroked her hair as it fell through his fingers. "My name is Sven. I have waited an eternity for a woman like you."

Everything about this strikingly attractive man including his French accent was eerily hypnotic. Sensation sizzled through Mona's body. Her lips trembled, and she swayed toward him. Around her, the world faded; she was aware only of him—his touch, his breath. The scent of him was intoxicating. Her lips parted seductively, whispering, "I'm Mona. I'll be at the Hotel Valencia tonight."

His primal and ancient survival instinct caused him to pause. A strange, uneasy feeling gripped him. Prickles at the back of his neck compelled him to straighten away from the woman. Danger lurked. He looked for . . . the Enforcer sent by the Council. Yes, that was it; he detected his scent.

Sven backed away as the fiery redhead approached.

Koleen snatched Mona's arm and jerked. "Earth to Mona, Earth to Mona."

Mona blinked several times and tried to clear her head as Koleen dragged her back to the van.

"You big dummy! You almost got yourself killed standing in the middle of this busy gas station. Didn't you hear that truck driver honk and yell things even I can't repeat? You just stood there totally oblivious to what was going on around you." Koleen stopped. Mona was staring at her, but her eyes seemed far way. Her face was very pale. Bright pink patches stained her cheeks. "Hey, are you okay? What was he saying to you anyway?" Koleen pushed Mona out of harm's way and slammed the van door.

Puzzled, Mona mumbled, "I don't remember, but I do know that I didn't want him to stop." She pressed her cheek against the window; it felt cool and soothing to her feverish skin. *Wow, that was intense*, she thought. *I bet he's hot in bed.* She hoped she had a chance at an erotic encounter with this glorious creature. This would be yet another opportunity to experience the exploding passion that most women only read about in those paperback romance novels.

Her husband had been a selfish, greedy bastard during their lovemaking. Only thinking about himself, he never once considered that she might have needs too. Foreplay was an eight-second bull ride. Resentment had built up over the years until . . . She let her thoughts drift back to that lethal night.

"He just wouldn't listen," Mona had cried. "He was determined to have the ultimate sexual experience: greater intensity and prolonged duration of the side effects of Viagra, including an erection lasting longer than four hours." She had collapsed into Officer O'Donnell's arms, pressing her 44-D breasts against his bulging chest. He had done what any decent, red-blooded male would have done. He gathered her close and held her until the fit of weeping subsided.

In a consoling whisper, he said the first thing that came to his mind, "Mrs. Dix, why would any man need Viagra with a woman like you in his bed?"

Officer O'Donnell reluctantly left the inconsolable Mona crying into his handkerchief when the paramedics arrived followed by the coroner.

Dominic nudged Mona, distracting her from the distressing memories. "Buckle up," she urged.

Mona did as she was asked. Turning to get a better grip on the seatbelt, she noticed the black Hummer. It looked almost sinister, sitting there at the pumps. She was sure the men had been following them for most of the trip. She knew she would be seeing Sven in San Antonio. It was going to be a long ride, but he would be worth the wait.

With a twinge of regret, Sven joined the others getting back in the Hummer. Still scanning the horizon for anything out of place, he leaned to the driver, "We're being watched. It's not safe here."

As the Hummer inched away from the station and headed for the freeway, the driver barked in disgust, "When are you going to learn to stop thinking with your dick? You just made a fatal mistake back there by telling that "piece of fluff" your real name! Now you are bound to her. You know the cardinal rule—NEVER under any circumstance divulge your true identity to a mortal!"

"Shut up and drive," Sven snarled. As tempting as this woman was, he vowed not let his hunger for her get in the way of his ultimate objective, the artifact.

His gang clung to the old way, which had been banned by the Elders. They were wanted with a bounty on their heads. Loathed and despised by their own kind, they were hunted by the Council's Enforcers. Thankfully, his man on the Council saw things the way he did. Possession of the book would just be the leverage he needed to end the unjust persecution his band of outlaws was fleeing from.

The Watcher knew the women were in danger from the sly wolves in the Hummer. The old vampires were savages that drank blood and ate the flesh of their victims, leaving a mutilated corpse. The redhead had managed to save one of the helpless lambs from the slaughter for now anyway.

Chapter 7

The Watcher had told the Elders that everything was under control, but that was far from the truth. Mind control had proven ineffective; the renegades were stalking the women, and the artifact was still in the possession of the redhead. The council had chosen him for this assignment because of his one hundred percent track record. This operation wasn't going to be the first black mark on his otherwise perfect record.

He studied "Red" as she stepped onto the balcony of the hotel. In two hundred years, he had never encountered this problem before: strong-willed women who seemed to openly flout their ability to defy mind control. He was willing to do whatever it took to get the artifact and be done with these reckless and unruly mortals. With all his effort, he concentrated one last time to take over her mind before he was forced to resort to more drastic measures.

K oleen ignored the flutters in her stomach and the tingling that swept over her skin as she made a hasty retreat from the room to the balcony.

She glanced down at the two lamp-lit parallel sidewalks along the banks of the San Antonio River. The network of walkways that wound and looped their way under the bridges one story below the street were lined with bars, restaurants, and shops.

Koleen needed a minute to clear her head after all the chaos. Taking off her black designer glasses, she leaned on the wrought iron railing that ran along the balcony. She absently touched the chain around her neck, rubbing her fingers over the gold key. *What a day!* They had gotten lost again. They had eventually convinced Raven to exit the freeway after passing the Towers of America for the third time. Despite short tempers, frayed nerves, and everyone giving directions at once, they had finally found Commerce Street and located the Hotel Valencia. Now, they were getting ready to go to some vampire bar Dominic had found on the Internet.

She replayed the drama that had forced her to flee the insanity of the room. Mona had thrown a fit when she discovered her pictures of the "Action Hero" hadn't turned out. The photos of the Hummer and the station were perfect, but her he-man, calendar hunk was missing. Dominic was trying to explain to Mona that the angle of the digital camera probably had something to do with it when Raven smirked, "Your he-man calendar was doomed to fail. You should have never made that 'Butts in the Snow' calendar without telling us. You should know that cheaters never prosper!"

Mona lunged at Raven, screaming, "You stupid bitch, if you messed with my camera, I swear I will kill you!"

"Is that what you said to your husband just before you . . ." was all Raven got out before Mona threw herself across the room with a murderous look in her eye.

Raven just laughed and deftly stepped aside as Jaylyn pinned Mona's arms behind her back.

Angel refereed. "Enough already, settle down. What's done is done; we can't go back and change the past. We've all been on edge today. Let's get ready for a night on the town. It's time to party!"

Disagreements and squabbles were inevitable regardless of efforts to skirt around certain topics, Koleen thought. The Mexico trip was a prime example. After drinking margaritas all afternoon, she had joined Mona, who was singing with the Mexican one-man band. Becoming too intoxicated to walk, she had been draped over Mona's shoulders like a sack of potatoes and lugged back across the border.

The next day, Mona drew a line in the sand. "I'm not dragging your ass all over Mexico again. You stick to beer for the rest of the trip!"

Traveling with these five women was never easy. Ruffled feathers and misunderstandings were nothing new, but this vacation had turned into a nightmare. It was more like the beginning of a scary movie. How in the world did I get talked into this nonsense? Vampires, wooden stakes, garlic perfume, baby tears, Mona with her sex toys, and that damn Real Man Calendar! Oh yeah, I could be curled up in my favorite chair with a good murder mystery novel. It was crazy. "Why do I continue to travel with the criminally insane?" she wondered aloud.

Flashing to the gas station incident, Koleen chuckled. Mona had been almost comatose when she had finally dragged her back to the van. Angel was certain Mona had caught the H1N1 virus because her face was so flushed and wanted to take her temperature. After digging around in her black satchel for several minutes, all she could come up with was a rectal thermometer. Seeing this, Mona tried to snatch it from Angel's hands and screamed, "Want me to show you what you can do with that instrument of torture?"

As they wrestled over the thermometer, Raven cranked up the radio, which was playing her favorite Willie Nelson song, "On the Road Again," drowning out Mona's irate screams and Angel's soothing nurse-like voice reassuring Mona over and over again, "Now, honey, this will not hurt one little bit." It finally came to an end when Jaylyn pointed out that Raven had just passed the San Antonio exit ramp.

Koleen's thoughts were interrupted when her eye caught a movement near one of the bridges. It was a man, the man from the airport. Tall and long-legged, his thick black hair hung to his broad shoulders. His eyes followed her every movement with the intensity of a predator. She wondered how long he had been there. He stepped back into the shadows as the other women spilled onto the balcony.

Koleen called out. "Wait," she said as he melted into the fading light.

She turned to the others. "Something really strange is going on here."

"Yeah, you're right," mocked Mona. "You're the only one not dressed for our first night on the town."

"No, no, really," Koleen tried to explain. The group ignored her protests and pushed her through the sliding glass doors into the room.

Koleen reached for the outfit Dominic tossed toward her. In a horrified voice, she declared, "I refuse to wear this!"

Eyes narrowing and lips pressed into a thin line, Dominic sneered, "Hell-oooo . . . , we're going to a vampire bar. We're playing a role here, and we have to look the part. Besides, I spent a small fortune on these. You're going to wear them and like it!"

"You're nothing but an obnoxious bully!" declared Koleen, looking at her friends standing uncomfortably around the room. She noticed they were all dressed in similar attire—black leather and fishnet stockings. The gold cross dangling from their necks was their only accessory.

Why had he let her see him? Had it been the scent of her blood? No doubt it had acted like a paralyzing drug, leaving his mind in a fog and affecting his judgment. His lips parted as a growl escaped from deep within his throat. The redhead had awakened a hunger in him. Now his mission had taken on a new urgency.

Chapter 8

The Watcher followed the women to the "Blue Moon," one of the most notorious vampire bars in San Antonio. Hoping for the best, he expected the worse.

Stumbling, Mona fell against Angel. "I'm breaking the heels off these son-of-a bitches the first chance I get."

Giving her a go-to-hell look, Dominic hurried ahead as they wobbled along behind in their six-inch knee-high stiletto boots. She turned, ran back to Koleen, grabbed her hand, and dragged her toward the entrance. "Do you hear that?"

"Yeah, you mean that eerie sound coming from the bar?" teased Koleen.

"It's the theme song from *Dark Shadows*," squealed Dominic. "Oh, this is so cool!"

Koleen rolled her eyes and motioned the others to follow. "I see you still haven't gotten over your teenage crush on Barnabas Collins, the two-hundred-year-old vampire from that dreadful sixties soap opera," taunted Koleen.

Their entrance was barred by a tall, muscular man with a shaved head and gold earring demanding a cover charge.

"Twenty-five bucks . . . just to see bloodsuckers?" Raven grumbled, digging in her purse.

Handing over two tens and a five, Raven muttered, "Whatever happened to the idea of cheap thrills?"

"For God's sake . . . It's all about the experience. Where's your sense of adventure?" asked Jaylyn.

"You're such a cheapskate, Raven. I bet you invented copper wire fighting over a penny," taunted Angel.

As the group entered, Baldy flashed them a smile. Wide-eyed, Koleen looked at Mona and mouthed, "Did you see the size of his incisors?"

Mona shook her head. "Fake, you can get those in the 'kiddy' department at any discount store!"

Darkness engulfed them; the six paused, allowing their eyes to adjust. Silhouetted by candlelight, patrons sat at tables and booths, chatting and sipping on drinks that glowed blood red. In one corner, a band, thin and pale and with extremely black hair, played next to an open wooden coffin. A mist of thick fog rose from the dance floor. It hovered and swirled about the couples, swaying to the beat of the dark lyrics belted out by the lead singer. "How can they dance to this crap?" complained Mona.

Dominic led the way to an empty booth near the band. The girls slid their butts across the slick vinyl as a petite Asian cocktail waitress approached. "What can I get you, ladies?"

"What's the house specialty?" requested Raven.

"A martini the proprietor has dubbed the *Vampire Kiss,*" was her bored reply.

"You've got to be kidding. Is that what's in the glowing glasses?" asked Angel.

"Yes, it's quite a popular drink in our establishment."

"It must be good," Jaylyn pointed out. "Looks like everyone in this joint is drinking the red concoction." With that, they ordered six of the martinis. They all agreed it was pretty damn strange, but as Jaylyn had said earlier, "It's all about the experience." Everyone admitted that the drinks added to the ambiance.

"It's probably synthetic blood," Dominic muttered.

Confused, Mona asked, "What the heck are you talking about?"

A single flickering candle stood in the center of the table. The flame illuminated Dominic's face as she leaned forward and coaxed the others into a secret huddle. "Through my research for our fantasy-reality vacation, I discovered that immortals . . . vampires, don't feed off the hoof anymore. To put it more politely, they don't bite and suck the blood of mortals. They have developed this synthetic blood to replace human blood. The Elders of the Grand Council, who rule the vampires, banned biting and feeding on humans. They believed the old ways of feeding had to be stopped for the safety of the realm. Feeding off humans was too risky. If mortals ever found out that vampires were real, it would cause a panic and ultimately lead to the fall of the vampire kingdom and their dark reign."

Seeing she had everyone's attention, Dominic continued, "The members of the Grand Council had sent out a decree. No hunting or feeding off humans except in extreme situations. In rare cases, vampires were allowed to take only enough human blood to sustain them until the Elders could send a shipment of synthetic blood. Mortal memories had to be erased so the victim wouldn't remember being fed upon."

Looking around the dark room, Koleen said nervously, "Well, it's a good thing we've been practicing that yoga mind training. Crap, if there are any vampires in here, they'll find that my mind is like a steel trap . . . Nothing gets in, and nothing gets out!"

"Hell, your mind's been like that for years," Mona chuckled.

The waitress returned with their drinks. Noting the strong resemblance the red liquid had to real blood, Mona looked up at her and smiled weakly. "I guess it's too late to change our order, isn't it?"

"Just try it, sweetie," she smirked as she took their money and went about her duties.

After Dominic's lecture on synthetic blood, the drinks sat untouched. "OK, we're here, so let's try to score some points for our game cards," Dominic insisted.

"I don't know," Jaylyn began uncertainly. "This place is really starting to give me the creeps. Everyone is watching us. Can't you feel it? What if there really are vampires, and we have invaded their territory?"

"Oh, don't be such a baby. Get up and mingle. What are you afraid of? You have your stakes, baby tears, and garlic perfume so what more could a vampire hunter need?" asked Dominic.

"How about courage?" wailed Jaylyn.

"I don't have a pill for that," Angel replied softly, shaking her head.

"Draw on your inner strength instead of stifling it. Use the yoga breathing techniques I taught you to quiet and control your mind," encouraged Dominic.

Startled, they turned as a deep male voice interrupted their argument. He held out his hand to Koleen. "Would you like to dance?" His old-world accent was barely detectable.

Koleen looked uncertainly around the table at the others who appeared to be as surprised as she was at the invitation. Without hesitation, they all answered for her, "Yes, she would."

Annoyed at the group's reaction, Koleen reluctantly placed her fingers in his hand and rose from her seat. The touch of his cool, smooth skin set off fireworks from her head to her toes. Her body was virtually humming with an odd, exciting tension.

The Watcher was surprised with his invitation; his intentions were to simply warn the women of the danger they were in. He drew her close. For a moment, he was transfixed by her slender athletic body. Usually, he preferred his women with a little more meat on their bones. Oddly, she felt so right as he pressed into her. He found women who wore glasses unattractive; he didn't like red hair, and he hated freckles. Astonishingly, the glasses just accentuated the emerald green of her eyes, her red hair shimmered in the candlelight, and to his delight, he found the freckles scattered across the bridge of her nose quite charming.

Her head came up just shy of his chin. Bending, he breathed her scent. The aroma of her hair reminded him of his homeland in the spring when the heather was in bloom on the moor. Clean, sweet, natural scents of her body wafted to his nose, stirring a hidden desire within him. Their bodies moved as one to the slow beat of the music. Centuries-old, he had experienced many women, but the countless were soon forgotten as he held Koleen in his arms. She was very tempting, and he had to remind himself he wasn't interested in a relationship with a mortal.

Koleen closed her eyes and let him pull her closer. He was a very good dancer. She had forgotten how much she loved to dance. She let the baggage of her failed marriage and the disappearance of her husband slip away. This was exactly what she needed to rebuild her self-esteem.

Koleen felt his breath, feather-light on her neck, tracing a moist, cool path to her ear. His tongue slipped along an invisible line to her pulse, which was beating erratically. It was deliciously exotic. When he started nibbling at her neck, Koleen thought she would have a meltdown right there on the dance floor.

Warning bells started going off. *Something wasn't right. Here was a gorgeous man, who could have any woman he wanted. Why me? What was he after?*

At first, he was confused. He shook his head to clear his thoughts. It took a minute to erase the titillating images that filled his head. Then, he realized she had stopped moving and stood glaring at him.

"It's all coming together," snapped Koleen. "You were at the airport, and I saw you watching us from the shadows. You were hiding under the bridge, spying on us again at the hotel. You were also at that estate auction, weren't you? It's not me you're interested in; it's that damn Vampire Bible! You're a lousy prick!"

Mouth agape then abruptly shut, he had no answer. He couldn't explain why he was following her without revealing the reason for his mission. Certainly, he couldn't explain what had possessed him to ask her to dance any more than he could explain what had just happened between them on the dance floor.

Jerking away from his hold, she stomped back to the table where she was met with looks of sheer disbelief.

He was sure he had just complicated his mission, but he still had to warn them. With quick steps, he followed Koleen to the booth. "Ladies, I must insist you leave this establishment as soon as possible. I'm telling you, this place is not what it appears to be. You have put yourselves in great peril by coming here."

"Hey, let's go," piped up Mona nervously. "This place is a drag anyway."

"Too late," Raven said, nodding with her head toward the bar. There, under the neon lights of a Budweiser sign, stood the six babes from the Hummer.

Why had he deviated from his mission? If only he had warned them sooner, they wouldn't be in the mess that was sure to unfold.

Chapter 9

The Watcher smelled the vampires before he saw them.

"**O**h, no! Trouble has arrived," Koleen said under her breath, yanking Mona's arm, warning her not to move.

Mona's lips curved into a seductive smile. Sven and his friends had just walked into the bar. It took every ounce of willpower to sit quietly until he noticed her. Dominic had tried to explain to her once before that men didn't like aggressive, pushy women. At the time, Mona had just thought Dominic was peddling more of her "useless Internet drivel" and had brushed her off. Mona, in return, had pointed out to Dominic that she didn't need any help with her love life. But in light of the fact that her last relationship hadn't ended well, Mona decided that Dominic's counsel worth considering. *I'll give it a try,* she thought, turning her back to the bar as Sven glanced her way.

What game was she playing by pretending she hadn't seen him? Hadn't his mind control worked at the gas station? Most mortal women found him irresistible. Could this woman be more than a meal? *Fascinating!* Sven thought.

The atmosphere crackled with static energy; the band had ceased their performance. Seated patrons, now silent, focused their angry glare on the six gathered at the bar. Smelling fresh human blood, the burly bartender bared his fangs and growled, "We don't serve your kind here. You've been feeding off the hoof. Get out!" The advice came too late.

As one, they turned to face the hostile vampire crowd, and then all hell broke loose. Chairs and tables flew through the air; customers ducked to avoid the devastating blows. Bottles ricocheted off walls. Glasses exploded, spraying red liquid over the fighting arena. Shouts of encouragement and howls of pain erupted throughout the bar. Terrified, the women shielded their faces from the flying debris.

Instinctively, Dominic jumped up from the table and moved into her "Eye of the Tiger" stance, ordering the other women to get behind her. "Bar fight tip number one: Show no fear."

"Is this more of your Internet research bullshit?" hissed Raven between her clenched teeth as the group inched their way backward toward the entrance.

"Why would we show fear? We are armed with garlic and baby tears against a bar full of pissed off what appears to be VAMPIRES!" screamed Koleen at Dominic.

"Yeah," piped in Jaylyn sarcastically as she ducked the chair that went flying over her head. "And we're being defended by someone who has received her black belt in tae kwon do after completing a six-week Internet course!"

Jaylyn held up her cross to shield whatever evil had been unleashed and encouraged the others to do the same. She yelled, "If this doesn't work, we're going to wake up tomorrow with teeth marks on our necks!"

"Oh yeah of little faith. You must heed the voice you hear in your heart, and if it leads you into darkness, trust that there is a reason," replied Dominic confidently as the hefty hunk with muscles thick as bricks approached ready to do damage. "I usually don't mess with anyone whose neck is bigger than their head; extreme circumstances call for extreme measures," she explained, positioning her hands for the first attack.

"That big brute is going to make lunch meat out of you!" Jaylyn shouted over the roar of the raging fight.

"Accuracy and speed are more important than pure power," Dominic replied as she swiftly karate-chopped the beefy neck of her sparring partner. He staggered backward, and she finished him with what she called her "Ass-Kicking Move." Leaping in the air, she spun around, planting the heel of her stiletto at an angle just below the ribs. The man teetered, hit the floor with a thud, and lay motionless. "I love liver shots," she smiled. "Wow, where did you learn that? Please, don't say off the Internet," pleaded Koleen.

"Ask me no questions, and I'll tell you no lies" was Dominic's answer. Clutching their gold crosses, the women backed through the entrance, spilling onto the street.

Raven yelled, "Run!" For once, they obeyed.

Jaylyn looked back in time to see the dark-haired man who had warned them. He punched the blond pursuing them, one of the six Hummer babes who had instigated the fight. Blood poured from his mouth, and a small gurgle of sound slid from his lips as he crumpled to the concrete sidewalk.

The Watcher knew the women's lives were still in jeopardy, but he now held out some hope for their safety. The women had proven that they weren't as helpless as he thought. At least, it appeared one of them had been training with a master of the martial arts.

Chapter 10

The Watcher lugged the unconscious renegade around the corner to the dark alley. He planned to follow the women as soon as the vampires from the Council's Special Opts Division collected the rogue. The bad boy would be hauled in front of the Elders. He would be given a choice—change his ways or be staked. It was clear that he was part of the rebel band that had been tracking the women. The rest of the gang had escaped during the fight, and they were probably in hot pursuit of the women. This was going to be a long night.

Rounding the corner, the shaken bar fight refugees collapsed on a well-lit bus bench. Even at night, crowds of tourists and locals walked along bustling Commerce Street, the main artery of San Antonio. Trolleys, city buses, and taxis whizzed by with passengers anxious to get to their destinations.

"You are without a doubt the craziest bunch I've ever run with!" gasped Jaylyn, trying to get her breath.

"So what if we are crazy? I still scored the most points!" exclaimed Mona, turning to her friends and waving her scorecard in the air.

"No way!" yelled Dominic, jumping up, stomping her foot, and lunging for the offending card. "I just saved your sorry asses! Give me that damn scorecard!"

"You might have helped save us, but no way did you get the most points!" Koleen chimed in. "The points, in my opinion, should go to me for being railroaded into dancing with that jerk!"

"Maybe you should be thanking that jerk," Jaylyn pointed out. "He did stop one of the thugs who seemed intent on following us."

"To hell with the points; I'm ready for a drink!" proclaimed Angel, noticing all the attention they were getting from people waiting for the next bus. "Let's try another bar."

"I'm with you," said Raven. "I'd say we need to celebrate being alive."

Finally in agreement, they sauntered down the street. "Look," pointed Raven. A flashing neon sign hung over a dark, open doorway. "There's the Boogie Boot Saloon."

"That's more like it, a bar that we've all heard of," smiled Jaylyn.

"Isn't that where women dance on the bar and leave their bras hanging in the rafters?" asked Dominic.

"Hell, yeah!" screamed Mona. "I want to shake my booty on that bar. How about you, Koleen?"

"Yeah, but I'm not leaving my bra; someone might mistake it for an eye patch!"

Waves of laughter erupted from the gang as they entered the bar. Koleen was always the butt of small breast jokes. Thankfully, she was good-natured about it.

The saloon first opened its doors to the public in the early nineties. It was an instant success with sassy bartenders who would stop work, clear off the bar, and jump up for a two-step. Tonight was no exception. A host of drinkers had flocked to the bourbon-and-beer joint to witness the young cowgirls performing. All social-economic groups were represented; they ranged from businessmen in suits to bikers in their traditional leather garb. Two young, sexy gals in frayed blue-jean cutoffs, halter tops, and boots were stomping to a wild, country-Western song, blaring from a corner jukebox.

"I want up there!" howled Dominic, running toward the bar.

Not to be outdone, Mona beat Dominic to the bar and whooped, "Me too!"

"Those two are headed for trouble," grinned Jaylyn, shaking her head.

Raven turned to the other women left standing at the door. "I'm having a drink first."

Wrinkling her nose, Angel insisted, "No **bloody** drinks this time."

"I'll get us a place to sit," Jaylyn said, motioning for the group to follow her to an empty table as Dominic and Mona squeezed for a place at the bar.

"Let's order a round of tequila shots to get us started," recommended Koleen as the group positioned themselves around the table to watch the action. Seeing the barmaid doing the two-step, Koleen headed for the bar. As she placed their order, a well-built dark figure eased to her side. He leaned in close to seductively whisper in her ear. The heat of his clean breath raced down her neck.

"*Por favor, mi Maria,*" he cooed.

She recognized him from the vampire joint. It wasn't her mysterious dance partner, but somehow he was equally attractive. Captured by his way and yet distracted, Koleen forgot what she was doing and replied, "Oh my God, is that Dominic and Mona on the bar?" Sure enough, they had done what they had set out to do. The two were stirring up the audience with a performance unlike any other.

The Watcher crossed the threshold of the open doorway and surveyed the crowd. Two of the women were dancing on the bar, three of them were sitting at a table, and that damn redhead was flirting with a vampire.

Chapter 11

The bar was rockin'. The place reeked of stale beer and testosterone. The near-fever-pitched frenzy of the crowd was being fueled by the women dancing on the bar. The Watcher shook his head. Damn, they weren't satisfied with causing a brawl at the vampire bar. Now, they were going to start a riot.

Focusing on the rogue approaching the dancers, the Watcher had almost missed the redhead being maneuvered down the dark hallway by another rogue vampire. Using his supernatural speed, he moved through the crowded bar undetected. He didn't stop to analyze his motive; he just acted on instinct.

Dominic let the music take hold. She swayed, waiting to catch the beat and then began undulating her hands and arms over her head. Rhythmic movements controlled her chest and abdomen. Flexing and contracting her stomach muscles, she thrust her hips to and fro like a Middle Eastern belly dancer.

Caught off guard by Dominic's sensual performance, Mona yelled over the whoops and hollers that erupted from the worked up audience, "You go girl!"

No doubt, it was probably something she learned from the Internet, Mona thought. *I'll show her a thing or two.*

With one hand, Mona grasped the slender pole near the end of the bar. Arching her body backward, she licked her lips and let her wild, wavy, long curls ripple over her shoulders. The exotic dance had attracted every man's attention including Sven and his band of rogues.

Standing in the corner, they had gone unnoticed. Sven fixed his hypnotic stare on Mona. She felt his gaze and met it with a bold, knowing smile. She allowed him to slip into her mind, filling it with his desires. Her hand glided up and down the pole. Leaning back, she descended into a squatting position as he commanded. Arching her upper body forward, she slipped seductively back up the pole, never taking her eyes from his.

To feel those glorious curves against him, under him, and around him was overpowering. Sven's manhood swelled beneath his tight-fitting jeans. *Was she worth the risk?* He pondered for one brief moment. *To hell with the risk!* Sven tossed back his head and drained the fiery whiskey, welcoming the burn as it coursed through his veins. His fangs lengthened as he weaved his way through the crowd of sweaty mortals.

Witnessing Mona's act, Dominic was determined to outdo her. Knees spread apart, legs swathed in fishnet stockings, she provocatively lowered her upper body to the bar in a backbend. Dominic jumped up, landing firmly on both heels of her black leather boots like a gymnast. Her shimmering finale was abruptly interrupted by an earth-shattering scream.

The screams steamrolled over him in searing waves that blistered his mind, making his head ache.

Chapter 12

The Watcher became one with the shadows of the bar. Damn, that was a close call! A few more seconds and the redhead would have been toast.

The blood-curdling scream echoed through the bar, drawing everyone's attention to the half-naked woman stumbling from the hallway. "Damn that Koleen!" Dominic swore. "She always has to be the center of attention." Dominic vaulted off the bar, landing in front of Koleen. Hurriedly, she covered Koleen's exposed breasts and led her back to their table. Seeing that the screamer had been rescued, the bar roared back to life.

Raven demanded, "What's goin' on here?"

Koleen sat like a deer caught in the headlights. "She's in shock!" Angel diagnosed.

"Give her a drink," prompted Jaylyn.

Angel held a shot of tequila to her lips, but Koleen didn't respond. Short-circuited with horror, she sat trembling. The unbelievable scene played back and forth like a pendulum. The handsome man had seduced her by kissing and licking her neck. He had diverted her attention from her friends dancing on the bar. Instinctively, he had known what turned her on. Using his firm hands to massage her shoulders and then possessively placing them on her hips was all it had taken to win her over. *How could she explain what had happened?*

Dominic slapped Koleen hard on the face. "Snap out of it!"

Blinking her eyes, feeling the sting, Koleen jolted back to reality and focused. "You're not going to believe what just happened!"

Urging Koleen to continue, the women leaned forward, straining to hear every word. "It's been months since I felt a man's touch and longed to do the wild thing," she began. "I shamelessly let the man at the bar take me to the ladies' room." The four women snickered but didn't interrupt her tale. "He coaxed me into the bathroom, and checked the stalls. He pinned me to the wall with one hand and threw the metal trash can against the door with the other."

"This is better than an X-rated movie," Angel admitted. "What happened next?"

"He pulled me to him until I stood between his legs, close enough to feel every muscle in his lean body. His incredible hands began to roam. I had no will to stop him. One hand cupped my breast while the other drifted over my stomach and up my skirt."

"Lordy, Lordy!" gasped Angel, fanning herself with a bar napkin.

Dominic held up her hand to stop Koleen. "We don't need to hear all the little sordid details. Just cut to the chase. How did you wind up half-naked?"

"He undressed me like a June bride. My panties steamed, and my crotch simmered; he made my entire body tingle!"

"He must have been one hell of a stud!" interjected Raven, eyes widening.

"Next, he teased me. His mouth took my lips in a brief, sensual kiss, then he broke away to tongue-lash my shoulder and neck. I was on sensory overload at that point. I begged him to take me."

Raven shook her head disgustedly. "You didn't really say 'take me,' did you? That's right out of some dime store novel."

"When he raised his head, my eyes fluttered open. What I saw scared me shitless. His mouth opened wide, exposing two of the biggest, damn canines I've ever seen! They would have put a German shepherd to shame! That's when I screamed."

"Holy crap!" exclaimed Jaylyn. "It's a wonder you're still with us. How did you manage to get away?"

"That's the weird part. Right when I thought I was headed for the "Great Spirit" in the sky, he gagged and staggered backward, revealing, the tip of a stake protruding through the front of his chest. His body disintegrated and fell to the floor. All that was left of my vampire assailant was a wooden stake and ashes. Stunned, I almost missed my dark savior melting silently through the door. I ran into the hall, but he had disappeared. Girls, this vampire shit is real!"

"How many tequila shots did you have?" Raven snorted.

"Look . . . I know what I saw!" Koleen paused, looking around the table. "Hey, where's Mona?"

"That's what I've been waiting to tell you," declared Dominic, impatiently tossing the broken chain and gold cross on the scarred table. "Mona has disappeared!"

The Watcher knew that the women would need his help yet again. His face clouded. In twenty-four hours, his mission had gone from securing the artifact for the Council to a search-and-rescue operation for mortal women. He stood and shook his head then brightened. If he worked it right, he could do both and wind up with the redhead as a bonus. Tempting.

Chapter 13

The Watcher kept the women under surveillance from the shadows.

"And don't come back!" warned the bouncer gruffly, as he rudely shoved the women out the door. It was a kick in the teeth to be thrown out. Especially since none of them believed that they were responsible for what had occurred. Defiantly, they evil-eyed the hulking doorstop.

Outraged, Angel jeered in their defense, "We're the victims here . . . Fatty!" She hated confrontations and usually preferred to wear the hat of peacemaker.

"Wow, I've never heard you be so verbally abusive. Let the scum sucker have it!" encouraged Jaylyn. "He needs to pop one of your deadly chill pills."

Revved up by Angel's uncharacteristic behavior, Jaylyn jeered, "Roll your spare tire over here, Chubby. We'll deflate it for you!" The idiot just stood there with his arms folded across his bulging midsection, ignoring them.

Dominic took charge, "Don't waste your breath on that tub of lard, girls. We've got bigger problems." She herded the four away from the bar and down the street. "We have to report this to the police."

"Report what . . . a murder and a kidnapping? How are we going to explain to the nice policeman that one of our friends was kidnapped by a sex-crazed vampire while our other friend was getting-it-on with another bloodsucker in the powder room?" blurted Jaylyn.

"She's right," argued Angel. "We can't involve the police. They'd put us in straight-jacket and throw us in padded cells! Besides, haven't you ever watched CSI? Twenty-four hours is the waiting period for reporting a missing adult. I don't think this is just a weird case of coincidence. That swarm of vampires has been pursuing us all day: on the freeway, at the station, in the vampire bar, and then at the Boogie Boot Saloon. Doesn't that seem pretty strange?"

Shaking her head in disgust, Dominic complained, "Who would have thought our hunks from the Hummer would turn out to be such 'real' vampire bad boys? Just confirms my new philosophy on men: They run in packs like wild dogs, and they're all no good, lying . . . conniving . . . low lives!"

"We can be grateful that the gang has two less members after tonight," added Koleen.

"It all boils down to what we have that they want? And let's be perfectly clear here. It's not our gorgeous bodies or our great intellect they're after. Plain and simple, it's the Vampire Bible," Dominic declared, turning to Koleen.

"Yeah," added a tearful Jaylyn. "Maybe it's the Vampire Bible they want, and they're going to hold Mona for ransom."

"Don't even go there!" warned Koleen. "No way am I trading my meal ticket for Mona. I have plans, big plans for that money. She got herself into this mess, and she can damn well get herself out!"

"How can you say that? She's your friend," insisted Jaylyn. "Seems like you should be a little more sympathetic; after all, you just had a life-threatening encounter with one of those bloodsuckers and found out firsthand the power of their hypnotic allure.

Brushing them off, Koleen said, "Mona is probably enjoying every minute of her captivity and would be pissed as hell if we tried to rescue her before she had her way with that unsuspecting vampire. He may have lived for centuries, but he has never in his lifetime met a 'man-eater' like Mona. He's the one who will need rescuing. If we wait long enough, he'll pay us to take her off his hands!"

"You are one money-grubbing, cold-hearted bitch!" declared Dominic. Our friend is probably lying dead in some alley with her throat ripped out!"

"The first forty-eight hours are the most crucial in a kidnapping," stated Angel adamantly.

"Hell-oooo . . . , we don't even know where to start looking! OK, maybe I am wrong here, but which one of you has your PI license?" demanded Koleen sarcastically.

Dominic started to raise her hand, when Koleen glared at her and threatened, "Don't you dare try to tell us you got a PI license from the Internet, or I swear I'll throttle you."

"I hate it when you act like this!" shrieked Dominic, balling her hands into tight fists at her side.

Half-listening, Raven took a pack of cigarettes from her pocket. "What a damn mess," she mumbled. With a flick of her Bic, she lit up, drew hard, and tilted her head up to exhale. After a few puffs, she flipped the cigarette to the sidewalk and crunched it under the pointed toe of her boot. "Come on. Let's go back to the hotel. I've got an idea."

What were they up to now? It was sure to be some harebrained scheme to rescue their friend.

Chapter 14

The Watcher concealed himself under the bridge across from the Hotel Valencia. Lights in the window indicated their return.

"You want us to do what?" demanded Dominic for the third time, standing toe-to-toe with Raven in the center of the sitting room.

"You heard me the first time. I didn't stutter," Raven replied curtly. Hands on hips, she eyeballed the others in an attempt to rally support. "I want to have a séance. My Cherokee ancestors believed that the world was intertwined with and presided over by the spirits of the once living. If we could contact Yowa, the 'Master of the Sprit World,' we might be able to convince him to help us find Mona. There is one problem with holding a séance though. If we do not close the portal correctly, it leaves a doorway for some real evil spirits, ghouls, and demons to enter our world."

Surprisingly, Raven appeared perfectly sane as she unveiled her plan.

Angel's eyes grew wide with panic. The idea of spending the evening with a bunch of malevolent ghosts was downright frightening. She began feverishly digging around in her black satchel. "How about we play it safe and just take one of these mind-expanding drugs. They will alter our consciousness, allowing us to become one with the cosmos. If Mona is out there, we will find her."

Are those legal? Koleen wondered, looking doubtfully at the bottles in Angel's hand.

Dismissing Angel's idea, Dominic began to poke holes in Raven's bizarre proposal. "I think you have overlooked two small details. Number one, séances are for raising the dead; and well, excuse me for bringing this up, but Mona's not dead! Two, we do not know how to hold a séance."

"Oh, you mean little Miss Computer Genius can't 'Google' and find the information for us?" goaded Raven.

"I see, my skills and knowledge are only important when they serve a purpose in one of your idiotic plots. You realize it always ends this way. I provide the group with some obscure piece of information that saves your worthless necks. Otherwise, I'm just some computer geek. Am I reading you right?" Not waiting for an answer, Dominic stomped off to the bathroom and slammed the door behind her.

Angel turned to Jaylyn, "You know she's right. We do tend to pooh-pooh her technology skills. Not all her information is useless. She did save us with her kung fu fighting at the vampire bar."

In absolute disgust, Raven gave Angel a scathing look as she began beating on the locked door. "Get out here, and help us save Mona from the jaws of death, or I swear I'll come in there and drag you out!"

Hearing the latch click, Raven stepped back. The door opened. Dominic, head held high, proudly walked back into the room.

"Now, are you going to help us save Mona or not?" Raven asked.

"Well, it's sort of ironic that during my last job, I did come across some information involving séances. I researched Harry Houdini and other great magicians of the last century. Houdini was interested in spiritualism and communication with the dead. Bess, his widow, held an annual Halloween séance, hoping to contact her beloved Harry. After ten years of no show, she put an end to the ritual by saying " . . . ten years is long enough to wait for any man.'"

Koleen jumped up. "Fine, but we are not waiting ten years for Mona; she has forty-eight hours to contact us, or she can join the ranks of the living dead."

Dominic warned. "A séance is an event that can either be fantastic or a real mess. It's too risky. We're already dealing with vampires; let's not push our luck by disturbing other nasty creatures from the underworld. Let's use something we know—meditation and yoga. It will free us from the boundaries of our minds, get us on the same wavelength as Mona, and allow us to read her thoughts.

"Sit on the floor in a circle. Get comfortable. Remove your shoes and loosen any confining clothing." Grunting and grumbling, everyone took their places cross-legged in a circle as Dominic demonstrated.

Once seated, Dominic wasted no time giving instructions. "We have to take this seriously. Our minds have to focus as one." Raising an eyebrow and directing her comment to Raven, she finished, "Anybody who is cynical or skeptical about the process will act as a broken link in the chain and destroy any chance we have of reaching Mona."

Regarding everyone in the circle, Dominic announced, "We need a personal item of Mona's. Personal possessions vibrate with the owner's energy and help accentuate the connection."

"I've got something in my purse." Koleen jumped up and started rummaging. "We all know Mona's trick of conning one of us into carrying her junk while making us think it's a privilege," she said sarcastically. A few seconds of searching and Koleen triumphantly passed a small velvet bag with a gold drawstring to Dominic.

Inside the bag, Dominic discovered a pair of police-issued handcuffs with a key. Dangling them from her thumb for the group to see, Dominic placed the cuffs in the center of the circle.

Jaylyn snickered, "Bet she'll miss those tonight."

"It's imperative that everyone follow my instructions to the letter. Sit close enough to hold hands, but not close enough to touch the other person's body. Close your eyes, relax every muscle, one by one. Now, focus your mind on breathing. Don't control the breathing, but witness it. As your body relaxes, your breathing will slow down. Your mind will become calm and quiet. Concentrate on breathing deeply until you feel our hearts synchronize and beat as one."

Clearing their minds, the five women focused. Within minutes, a single long, deep sound resonated and filled the room. "Ooooommm." The wave of energy produced above the circle vibrated like the heat rising from black asphalt on a hot summer day. Psychic energy waves intensified and rippled through time and space as their minds joined. A vision appeared in their shared mind's eye. They had done it. They had found Mona.

Finally, one by one, the light in each room was extinguished. Waiting a few more minutes and not detecting any movement, he decided they had given up on rescuing their friend and called it a night. That was the first sensible thing they had done all day. He turned and hastened down the sidewalk. Sunrise was approaching.

Chapter 15

The Watcher entered the elegant town house, strode across the immaculate, white carpet, and peered over the River Walk. Time was slipping away. He needed to report the kidnapping to the Council before sunrise. Hitting speed dial on his cell phone, he waited.

Backed against the wall, Mona was now facing three crouching vampires. A single shard of moonlight fell on their hungry faces from the boarded-up window. Red eyes glared, fangs bared, they inched toward her. Low, rumbling growls erupted, signaling an attack.

Paralyzing fear consumed her. Mona's legs buckled, sending her to the floor.

Sven intervened by blocking the three bloodthirsty beasts advancing on Mona. "She's mine!" His authoritative voice echoed in the dark dungeon-like room, freezing all movement.

"We're hungry!" They howled in protest.

"I'm in charge here. I have claimed her as mine. I'm telling you, feed elsewhere. The River Walk is just beyond these walls. Go feast on some unsuspecting tourist!" Sven roared.

Challenging his power, the taller rogue hissed a warning, "Don't YOU forget our objective here. We've lost two of our best warriors chasing this whore you've been sniffing after."

The rebellious trio scattered as Sven snarled and lunged at them. "Get out! I'll deal with you later!"

Reluctantly, they disappeared into the shadows. Silent, furious, and hungry, the bloodlust drove them in search of easy prey.

"Now, where were we?" Sven's eyes pinned the trembling Mona.

She silently considered her options. *Run . . . No, that would be a deadly mistake. Surely, one vampire would be much easier to handle than the three lurking outside.*

He stepped near, lightly resting his hands upon her shoulders. "Your heart is racing. Are you afraid to be alone with me?" Something playful yet dangerous ran beneath his words.

Remaining perfectly still, head bent, eyes closed, Mona contemplated. She was an avid conservationist and knew the danger of making eye contact or sudden movements when confronting a hungry wild animal on the prowl. "It would be foolish of me to not to be afraid," she breathed.

He gripped Mona's chin, forcing her head up. "Don't make the mistake of assuming that since I came to your rescue, you're safe. After living for centuries, I harbor no human feelings of compassion, love, or guilt."

Mona shivered as his hands slid to the small of her back and pressed her hips firmly against his erection. She realized the balance of power had slightly shifted in her favor. His desire and lust, dead and buried for decades, awakened. A fatal flaw she could turn to her advantage.

Easing his hand from the shallow of her back, Sven expertly located one of the obstacles standing in his way. With one soft pinch, he unhooked it. Mona's mountains tumbled free, exposing the firm peaks of her nipples. The other hand slid from her thigh up under her leather vest and squeezed a soft mound. Finding the nipple, he teased. He clamped the hardened bud between his thumb and finger. A murmur escaped from her parted lips as he increased the pressure and pressed his hard, swollen crotch against her.

His lips moved from her forehead down the bridge of her nose, capturing her mouth. As the kiss deepened, Sven's hands made quick work of Mona's buttons and zippers. Her clothing slipped to the floor. She stood in her six inch stilettos realizing her predicament a little too late; she was about to have unprotected sex with a vampire. No gold cross, garlic perfume, wooden stake, or worse . . . handcuffs. Mona was literally standing at death's doorstep. *Time to choose a different weapon.* Switching gears, she went from helpless victim to seductive slut. She clawed at his tight-fitting jeans; they loosened as she yanked open the button-fly barrier. Mona cupped and squeezed his buttocks. "No underwear, yum . . . ," she purred. Playing his sex game, she shucked his jeans to the floor. Rising, Mona arched her back and rocked against his erection.

Ankle-cuffed by his Levis, Sven was in a heated frenzy. Toe-to-heel, he quickly raked free of his boots. Squirming, he escaped from the bonds of his clothing. With ease, he swept Mona up. Continuing her role of seductress, she licked her lips and smiled at him. Reining in his hunger, Sven carried Mona to his bed and placed her gently on the soft, white cushions of the open coffin. He climbed in, settling next to her.

Leaning close, he braced his hands on either side of her. His sleek, hard body looked like it had been chiseled by Michelangelo from polished stone. Mona stared into his eyes, inches from hers. The cool feel of his rock-hard chest and thighs was a welcome relief to the fire he had ignited.

"Don't be afraid. I promise you, this will be one night you won't soon forget." He smiled, lowered his head, and roughly devoured her lips.

His hands slid up her thighs over the round warmth of her belly. Drifting downward, he spread her thighs, parting the wet folds to stroke her throbbing clit. One, then two fingers penetrated and stretched her inner flesh. Wet with Mona's essences, they dipped in and out.

"Take me . . . Take me NOW!" she begged.

"Hush. We've got plenty of time. Remember, I'm the one in charge here."

Mona dug her nails into Sven's back as the "Bad Boy" sucked and nipped on her breasts. He had a voracious appetite for what was lying, waiting for him between her legs. Craving the musky nectar of her creamy center, his mouth blazed a trail of heat to her love triangle. Nestling his head in her warmth, Sven began his sweet torture.

"Oh, my God!" she moaned in a husky voice. "Oh . . . Baby . . . Please . . . Don't stop!"

In a moment of weakness, Mona let down her mental guard and concentrated solely on the desire unleashed by his commanding tongue. As the wall fell away, the psychic energy unleashed by the sisterhood entered and merged with Mona's.

Back in the darkened hotel room, a moan escaped from each of the women's mouths, matching the cries of tormented pleasure from Mona. Their collective whimper echoed in her mind.

Her eyes flew open. *They are in my head! Those dirty bitches are using me as some kind of guinea pig in a mind control experiment.* Mona offered the only logical response. Her long, low scream of rage filled the night.

Calm down. We're only trying to save you Their voices meshed as one. *Tell us where you are, and we will leave.*

Can't talk . . . life or death . . . fuck or die situation . . . trying to tame a savage vampire. Mona's thoughts were cutting in and out like a cell phone with a bad connection.

The voice took on urgency, warning her of impending danger. *This is not a game, Mona. He's a vampire; you're dinner! He's only playing with his food.*

Sighing in exasperation, Mona relented, *. . . boarded up abandoned . . . River . . .*

Shaking her head in protest, Mona's frustrated scream broadcast loud and clear, *Get out of my head!*

Retrieving the mini bits of jumbled information, they withdrew from her mind.

Mona's scream stirred Sven's hunger, and a guttural growl ripped from deep within his core. He struggled to contain his fiery need. Gripping her hips, he buried the length of his shaft. Slow and hard, he pumped. Controlling his need no longer, he thrust harder and faster.

Mona gasped and writhed beneath him. *He was huge!* His massiveness set off multiple ripples of fulfillment throughout her body. No man had gone this deep or given her such gratification. Her hips rose to meet his driving force. "Impale me, baby." He obeyed her desire.

Mona's muscles contracted, releasing her coiled tension in a tidal wave that sent Sven over the edge. Succumbing to his intense rhythm, she was unaware of the fangs piercing the pulsing vein below her ear. He drank long and deep, feeding on her sweetness. Bloodlust finally satiated, he continued punishing her with his powerful pounding. His lower body jerked forward; his head flew back. He erupted like a volcano spewing his hot seed inside her.

Slick from the heat of their passion, Sven collapsed, covering Mona's quaking aftershocks. One thing was for certain—the feeling of boredom that usually came on the heels of a successful hunt and conquest was absent. He brushed a silky strand of hair from her neck and gently licked away the remaining droplets of blood. Protectively, he held her as he reached to lower the coffin lid.

Exhausted, Mona slipped into sleep, her last conscious thought was, *I survived!*

The Watcher hung the "Do Not Disturb" sign on the door, closed the heavy drapes, and climbed into bed. He would continue his quest for the artifact under the cover of darkness.

Chapter 16

The "sleep of the dead" left the Watcher defenseless as he lay stretched out in the darkened suite. During this deathlike trance, he was aware of the outside world but unable to move. Sunrise to sunset was a vulnerable time for vampires; a mortal's attack would be a death sentence.

"Excuse me," Koleen got the receptionist's attention. "Time is money. I can't be sitting around here all day! I did have an appointment!" Koleen's impatience was fueling a murderous rage. Thankfully, she perceived its onset and reigned in the brewing storm. "Can you tell me when Mr. Eastman will be out of his meeting?"

Nonchalantly, the blond bimbo squeaked, "I don't ever know how long his meetings will take. Mr. Eastman doesn't like to be interrupted."

Koleen and Dominic had waited on the thirteenth floor of the Eastman Office Building, watching tourists mill in and out of the Alamo for nearly an hour. Letting her irritation show, Dominic said tight-lipped, "I'm glad you decided not to lug that stupid book all the way over here because it looks like Eastman has given you the shaft."

"I'm not stupid. With something this valuable, I wanted to see if he was on the up and up . . . this is just a preliminary meeting," Koleen replied, gritting her teeth.

Unable to control her sharp tongue, Dominic lashed out, "Mr. Oilman has kept us in this holding pattern long enough! Let's leave. We were supposed to meet Jaylyn, Raven, and Angel at the convention center twenty minutes ago."

Muffled male voices and gruff laughter filtered from the inner sanctuary of the office suites. Without warning, the massive mahogany doors guarding the entrance opened. The blond glanced at his Rolex, signaling an end to the meeting. He now turned his glacier-blue eyes to Koleen and Dominic. Lean and tall, he boldly approached them.

Eastman didn't like doing business with women. They were unpredictable and unstable in his view. He liked his gals naked and in his bed where they could be controlled and used for one thing—his pleasure. Definitely, he didn't like mixing the two.

Dominic couldn't resist his magnetism. Bronze and weather-beaten, he carried himself like a cowboy from a John Wayne movie. Lifting one eyebrow, he smiled a warm, unguarded, welcome. "Hi, I'm Derek Eastman," he said, using his sexy Texan drawl.

"Hello, I'm Koleen O'Brien. I'm here about the artifact."

"Wonderful, and who is your charming friend?"

"I'm Dominic St. James."

Derek silently thanked the gods for delivering this delicious dessert right to his office. Dominic reminded him of a tasty ice cream treat—her smooth, creamy skin, shoulder-length caramel hair, and to top it all off, sweet cherry lips good enough to eat. With the confidence of a man who knew what he wanted and how to get it, he extended his large hand to Dominic.

Dominic noticed and thought, *Huge hands . . . Mona with her infinite knowledge of the male anatomy had once confided that this meant something else was rather large.* She offered her hand and was surprised when he gave an obvious squeeze before letting go. "Please, step into my office," he said, flashing his pearly whites.

Derek Eastman, a man used to being in charge, steered the women across the plush carpet. The office oozed masculinity. Two oversized leather chairs were placed strategically in front of the enormous mahogany desk that dominated the room. The library behind the desk displayed an extensive collection of first editions. Track lighting showcased art exhibits and his collection of rare, paranormal artifacts.

The cathedral ceiling gave the room a light, airy atmosphere. The beautiful oil paintings of the Alamo battle of 1836 added dramatic color. Koleen stepped to examine them. She was shocked by the bloody, graphic detail that was clearly visible upon close inspection. As Koleen studied the paintings, Eastman inspected Dominic.

Koleen and Dominic sank in the mammoth chairs. Derek perched himself on the top edge of his desk, legs sprawled facing them. His silver rodeo-sized belt buckle sparkled with diamonds. It called Dominic's name. In an instance, her gaze became an elevator. It left his buckle and descended to his lengthy legs, stopping at his silver-toed boots. Going back up to the first floor, it stuck when it hit the bulge in those tight-fitting jeans. *Damn,* she thought, *Mona was right—big hands . . . a big dick!* Hormones sizzling to life, she fought the urge to reach out and touch him.

Derek cleared his throat, signaling that the ride was over. Breaking her stare, she looked up and met the Texan's eyes; he had been watching her.

With a lopsided grin, he winked. *Maybe I can mix business with pleasure after all,* he thought.

Dominic blushed and silently scolded herself. *This is the worst possible time to become distracted by a man. True, he is good-looking, successful, and wealthy.* More her type than the other men she had encountered on this trip. Besides, it wasn't like she had men beating down her door. She was reluctant to risk getting tangled up in another relationship that might turn out like the one she had with her cheating commercial pilot husband. Catching him had been worth it though. Cab ride to the swanky hotel . . . $50. Bribe for the bellhop . . . $100. Look on her husband's face caught with his pants down around his ankles, pouring the pork to a stewardess bent over the couch, blue skirt hiked up around her waist . . . PRICELESS!

Abruptly, Derek pushed away from the desk, bringing Dominic back to the present. "Let's get down to business. I would like an opportunity to examine the book and box before we close the deal. If it checks out, you'll get your money, and I will get a relic for my museum," he declared triumphantly.

Derek held his arms wide, passionate about his new business deal. "It will draw tourists from all over the world and be a boom to this economically strapped city. The Vampire Bible will be the main attraction!"

Koleen and Dominic stole a glance at each other as Derek began pacing, consumed by his new capitalistic venture. In silent agreement, they acknowledged. Derek had been bitten by the vampire bug.

Warming to his subject, Derek proceeded to explain the reasoning behind his scheme. "In the new millennium, the line between fantasy and reality has become blurred in people's minds. The public has become fascinated by the interconnections of science, spirituality, and the supernatural. They look to modern science for feasible explanations for the existence of vampires, witches, ghosts, and any other legendary characters."

His pacing ended as he continued eye to eye with his visitors. "In the last decade, the United States has become the vampire capital of the world. The American media has romanticized the vampire's sexual allure; a majority of our youth are involved in the vampire lifestyle. There are even 'Fangfans' who dress in black, consume drinks designed to look like blood, and are obsessed with vampire novels and movies." Pointing to the rows of books behind his desk, Derek carried on with his soapbox lecture. "Scholars are re-examining ancient vampire myths and legends trying to separate fact from fiction. Scientists are scrambling to explain the vampire condition: genetic disorder, sickness of the blood, or the possibility of an entirely new species that are the result of genetic mutations."

He further explained, "My investors believe that the Vampire Bible holds all the secrets of the world of the undead. It will bare all the mysteries and mechanics of the paranormal. The ancient origins of the vampire race will be revealed along with the hidden purpose behind their civilization."

Dominic wanted to cover her eyes and pull her legs in close to her body. *Please make it all go away*, she quietly begged. *Had every single person in San Antonio descended into this vampire madness? It was disturbing to think that such a normal-appearing person could be so, well . . . deranged.*

Determined to put an end to the ranting and raving of the psycho cowboy, Koleen held up her hand and smiled. "I am convinced your museum is the perfect place for the artifact."

Sitting down at the desk, Derek flipped though his day planner. "I met earlier today with the museum's investors from the Dracula Society of Europe. They are presenting at the vampire conference I'm sponsoring. They plan to return to Europe at the end of the week. I would like to close the deal on the Bible before they leave. We have our eye on one special piece of property located on the River Walk. Once I have verified authenticity of the artifact, we are ready to break ground for the museum."

Red flags went up when the Texan mentioned the River Walk. Alarmed, Koleen stole a quick glance at Dominic. *Could Mona's kidnapping be part of some diabolical plot? This had to be more than a mere coincidence,* she thought to herself.

Reaching into his desk, Derek produced several passes to the convention. "Be my guests at the convention. I think you will find it very enlightening," he said in his smooth, twangy Texan accent.

The meeting concluded with Koleen agreeing to bring the artifact to Derek's office the next day for inspection.

Derek rose and escorted them to the door. Placing her hand on the ornate handle, Koleen paused and turned to Derek. "Just a friendly warning: the forces of spiritual darkness are nothing to trifle with. Vampires do exist, no matter what the so-called scientific, modern minds might say, and they ARE dangerous!"

Eyes flamed open; the Watcher snarled, exposing elongated fangs. That redheaded mercenary was determined to sell the sacred artifact, and worse . . . a treacherous Texan was willing to buy it! This could not happen and wouldn't! He was seized by the death sleep till dusk. His fury intensified.

Chapter 17

Even in his death sleep, the Watcher continued to track his target. The steady rhythm of her heart called to him like an African ceremonial drum. With each beat, the surge of blood filled her with life. He felt the pull . . .

Koleen and Dominic entered the convention center behind schedule. A maze of vendor booths and people hindered them as they searched for their friends. Remembering her cell phone, Koleen rang Angel.

"Aw, the power of technology," Dominic commented.

The meandering trio agreed to meet them at the front door. Once assembled, Dominic conveyed her theory, "I'm telling you, we are pawns in some type of supernatural conspiracy. Cowboy Eastman purposely detained us. I don't trust him; he's up to no good!"

"That's your excuse for keeping us hanging . . . a conspiracy?" I almost smoked an entire pack of cigarettes wondering if you two had been carried off by one of those walking corpses!" Raven vented hotly. "What a vacation this has turned out to be! Playing your fantasy vampire game has led to a sinister reality. Now you tell us you think we're involved in some kind of vampire plot!

"You're damn right; I believe it's a diabolical scheme of some sort!" Dominic contended. "Let's connect the dots. Koleen buys an old, moldy book at an auction. We are stalked by a pack of hungry vampires. Koleen is mistaken for a willing blood donor. Mona is kidnapped and turned into a sex slave. We meet an oilman who is a collector of gruesome and macabre artifacts. Lastly, a foreign vampire society is presenting at this very convention, trying to garner support for a paranormal museum on the River Walk. Can't you see? This is more than a fluke."

"You're incredibly sick!" exclaimed Raven. "Do you know how crazy you sound? You probably believe in UFO sightings, alien abductions, and a government cover-up of reported terrestrial landings in the New Mexico desert."

Observing Dominic's readiness to answer, Raven interjected, "PLEASE, don't answer that!"

"We're wasting time here, what about Mona's rescue?" Angel impatiently questioned.

"First, we need to locate the European Dracula Society's booth and find out exactly where this museum will be located," instructed Koleen.

"That shouldn't take too long," Jaylyn stated. "We've already been in four of the six exhibit halls. I didn't see that booth in any of them."

Angel and Raven confirmed Jaylyn's observations with a shake of their heads.

"Excellent detective work, ladies. Now, which two are left?" inquired Koleen.

Jaylyn pointed out the unexplored exhibit halls; they were numbered.

"OK, here's the plan," commanded Koleen. "Jaylyn, Angel, and Raven, you guys check hall number five. Dominic and I will get number six. Let's meet back here in an hour."

Dominic and Koleen's search yielded valuable information. They now knew the museum site and had acquired some interesting history about the Vampire Bible. As the two examined their find, they were interrupted by the rest of the search party. Dominic and Koleen's eyes widened in disbelief as the others descended on them. The three had clearly been on a shopping spree. Their arms were loaded with bags, boxes, and totes.

"Look what I bought!" exclaimed Jaylyn excitedly. The gold chain hanging from her neck had a miniature teardrop-shaped pendant designed with a removable sterling—silver cap. "It supposedly contains real vampire blood." Brushing her blond hair back, Jaylyn showed off her matching earrings. "I just had to have these too!"

Dominic shivered in horror as Angel opened her mouth, exposing lifelike fangs. They were relieved when Angel explained she had been fitted with removable vampire canines. She held up a small black box. "Look, they came in their own cute little coffin."

Raven approached, batting her eyelashes. They were prepared for more bizarre vampire souvenirs and weren't disappointed. If the eyes were truly the windows to a person's soul, Raven was in big trouble. Her irises were solid black with flames of hellfire blazing around the edges. "What the . . ." began Koleen.

"Cool, aren't they? For three hundred and ninety-nine bucks, you guys can get a pair of these hand-painted lenses. Look what else I picked up. Limited edition, it's 'Funeral Parlor' scent." Unscrewing the cap, she waved the black bottle under their noses. "Isn't it simply to-die-for? After the original fifty bottles are sold, that's it, no more," announced the fortunate Raven.

"Hey, the cheapskate turned loose of some green without whining for once," mocked Jaylyn sarcastically.

"Unbelievable . . . simply, unbelievable!" screamed Dominic. "We weren't here to shop." Jealous, Dominic secretly wished she had picked up another pair of fishnet stockings.

"We were trying to find the location of the museum . . . you know . . . help Mona!" Koleen emphatically reminded them.

"She didn't seem to want our help last night," said Angel, proudly flashing her new dentures.

"That was last night. I'm sure the reality of her position has set in this morning. Wait until she wakes up in a coffin with a vampire. She'll be singing a different tune," Dominic assured them.

Angel leaned toward Raven. "I don't know about that. I think one night with THAT vampire and . . . ," she snapped her fingers, "instant addiction!"

Waving several colorful brochures, Koleen proclaimed, "At least, some of us were thinking of Mona and not cheap vampire trinkets!"

Opening one of the pamphlets, Dominic pointed to a map. "Here's what we learned. Beginning in the eleventh century, the people of Western Europe launched a series of armed expeditions or Crusades to the Middle East. During the conflict, the armed forces led by a military order of knights confiscated hundreds of religious relics. One was an ancient scroll. Unknown to the Crusaders, the relic was the main channel for the supernatural power of a secret sect of vampires."

Taking the pamphlet from Dominic's hands, Koleen continued the story. "Eventually, the relics made their way to Western Europe, and the vampires followed. Ravaging country after country in their quest for the scroll, the vampire legend grew and spread throughout Europe."

"Here is where WE enter the story," Koleen said, looking over the top of her glasses. "For centuries, the scroll lay buried among other relics at a monastery in France. A monk found the scroll and began deciphering the ancient writing. Realizing the magnitude of his discovery, he smuggled it out of the monastery and sold it to a member of the royal family. To disguise the appearance of the scroll, it was bound as a book. During the French Revolution, the book was again smuggled, this time to the New World. Here it remained, lost to the world, until I posted it on eBay."

Exiting the center and walking down the sidewalk, Dominic realized that she had a tagalong. Dominic looked down upon a small dark-haired Mexican boy. With a slight accent, he whispered, "Madam Zorba has a message for you. *Beware; the power of the book calls to the Lords of Darkness.*" Pressing a card into her hand, he vanished into the busy crowd. She glanced at the simple white card. "Fortune-Telling and Spiritual Consultation" was scrawled across the top followed by an address and phone number.

His altered state foretold Gypsy Magic, and he hated dealing with mystics that dabbled in the dark arts.

Chapter 18

Trapped in the death sleep, the Watcher's mind raced. Witchcraft . . . sorcery . . . black magic.

Frustrated, Jaylyn threw her hands in the air, "We're lost again, aren't we? Give me that damn map!"

With both hands on the wheel, Raven let the implied criticism pass. She concentrated on the rearview mirror. They were on a lonely stretch of highway void of traffic. Gratefully, the sensation of being followed was absent today. *Maybe, the vampires were snoozing, gathering strength before they moved in for the kill tonight.* She shivered at the thought.

Doubtful, Raven asked, "Are you sure this is the correct address?"

"Yeah, check for yourself," answered Dominic, passing the card over the seat.

102

Briefly scanning the card, Raven signaled and turned off the two-lane highway onto an unpaved road. Gripping the seats, they braced themselves as the van jolted from side to side. Raven cursed, swerved, and tried to dodge the biggest potholes littering the bumpy dirt road.

Mesquite trees and cactus dotted the bleak terrain, a reminder of how far they were from civilization. Following the bend in the road, they spied a dilapidated homemade sign. "Zorba" and "Fortune" were the only distinguishable words left on the faded wooden marker. The van left the road and turned down a rutted lane running parallel to a sorry-looking one-story house. Peeling yellow paint and a sagging porch told a story of better times. Seven black hens pecked and scratched furiously in the dirt of the unkempt, weed-choked yard.

"Looks like the recession has really hit the magic industry pretty hard," said Angel taken aback by the squalor.

"It doesn't look like anyone lives here," added Dominic.

Koleen pointed to a red neon sign flashing "Open" in the cracked window. Silver duct tape zigzagged the window's scars, holding it together.

Sucking in a deep breath, Dominic asked in a hopeful voice, "Any volunteers?"

Koleen and Jaylyn took a second look at the house and yard and in unison firmly said, "No!"

Raven reminded Dominic, "I'm the driver. From the looks of the place, I had better keep this vehicle revved. We may need to make a speedy get-away."

Angel was fast to point out, "Hey, that kid gave you the card and warning. The way I see it, the fortune-teller wants a private session with you. Besides, our presence would just screw up the psychic vibes."

Reluctantly, Dominic lifted her hands in surrender. Sighing, she slid the door open and scooted out. Angel quickly slammed the door to a sudden close.

"We'll keep the air on. It's hotter than hell," mouthed Koleen as she fanned herself through the closed window.

"BITCH!" Dominic mouthed back. *Damn it*! Dominic wanted to scream. *Summers are hot; San Antonio with temperature of ninety or higher was famous for its killer heat waves*. That bit of information might not be appreciated right at this moment. Everyone was pretty tense.

She turned on her heels and cautiously approached the front doorstep. All eyes in the van and two from the broken window watched her progress. Screams of horror went up when an extremely large ferocious Rottweiler appeared. Teeth bared and jaws snapping, he raced toward Dominic. His head snapped back as he reached the end of his chain, halting just inches from the steps leading to the porch. The black devil stood on back legs, front feet pawing the air and foaming at the mouth. He snarled, gnashing his teeth in a desperate attempt to break free. Dominic turned to stone, unable to make a decision, *Van . . . Porch . . . Which is closer?*

Rolling down the van window, Raven yelled, "Get your scrawny ass on the porch. He looks serious!"

Dominic bounded up the three rickety wooden steps to the porch. Unnerved, she raised her fist to knock on the faded blue door. After the second round of knocking, she heard shuffling footsteps. The door cracked open, slightly revealing a pair of icy, cold eyes.

"Are you . . . Madam Zorba?"

"What do you want?" the old woman asked suspiciously.

Dominic slipped her the card.

Opening the door wider, a claw reached out and snagged Dominic's arm. Pulling her across the threshold, the door slammed shut. Heart in her throat, Dominic stifled a scream. *Get a grip*, she warned herself.

In a frail, Eastern-European accent, she beckoned Dominic to follow.

Dominic had to admit that she definitely looked the part of a fortune-teller. Golden hoops dangled from her ears, long ropes of colorful beads hung from her neck, and rows of silver bangles jingled on her arms. Undoubtedly, when it came to jewelry, she adhered to the philosophy "more is better."

Her long black skirt and white peasant blouse was tied at her waist with a scarlet sash. Adding drama to her outfit and really giving her the gypsy look was the eye-catching scarf wrapped around her head and secured in the back with a knot. Her shoulder-length, gray-white hair billowed out behind as she walked down the narrow, unlit hall toward a flickering candle.

Offering Dominic a chair at the round table in the center of the darkened room, the fortune-teller sat across from Dominic. Candlelight danced across her lined face. Her eyes pierced Dominic's soul. "You're filled with anguish, haunted by the shadows of your past."

A tremor waved under Dominic's damp T-shirt. She wondered, *Was this the usual spiel given to unsettle customers, or did the old woman really suspect something?* Careful not to give away her inner turmoil, Dominic held out her hand. "But you didn't read my palm or anything."

Fixing Dominic with a bone-chilling stare, Madam Zorba replied, "I don't need to. It's written all over your face."

"This is not about me. You sent me a message. I'm here to get some answers." Dominic did not want to her secrets discussed openly.

Focusing on the heart of the yellow candle flame, Zorba seemed to fall under its spell. While the wick sputtered and flared, Dominic glimpsed movement out of the corner of her eye. *Was it a shadow cast by the candle or was someone or something in the room? Had the witch conjured up a dead spirit?*

A singsong whisper escaped through the old woman's lips. "Darkest truths are made known; deadliest enemies are revealed. Evil lurks on the River Walk; she dances with death." With a shudder, her wobbly head fell face-down on the table. The thud of her forehead echoed in the stillness.

Heart racing, Dominic jumped up, knocking the chair backward. *Oh God, I've killed her!* she thought.

Reaching out with a trembling hand, Dominic gently prodded the body with the tip of her finger. She was taken by surprise when the old woman sat up. With a drawn-out sigh, the gypsy collapsed in her chair. An unsteady hand waved Dominic closer. "*El Mercado* . . . Charlie," she gasped between breaths.

Her last words to Dominic were, " . . . Need . . . silver bullets . . ."

SILVER BULLETS! The Watcher jolted to attention.

Chapter 19

Crossing the line between the day and night was a blur. The Watcher grew impatient as twilight approached. The situation with the women was escalating. That crazy gypsy had turned them on to the powers of silver. It was a deadly poison! Shot in the heart, a vampire would die instantly. If they were just wounded or a silver chunk lodged in them, the poison would spread. Their condition would rapidly deteriorate ending in death if not tended to. A gun loaded with silver bullets was a vampire's worst nightmare. Surely, these women didn't have a gun, did they?

"Welcome to Market Square. San Antonio's most unique and exciting shopping, dining, and entertaining experience," announced the trolley driver as he pulled over to stop.

The five women clamored to their feet and filed out behind the rest of the tourists. Crossing the street, they entered a colorful world that sang its own tune. Shops and restaurants, a blend of cultural and ethnic influences of Texas and Mexico, lined the main pedestrian walkways.

Hauntingly, tranquil sounds of a Peruvian flute drew them to the heart of the market.

Mesmerized, they gathered with the crowd in front of the raised landscape garden where the lone musician performed. Expert lips drifted across the tops of the thirteen different lengths of bamboo tubes bound together by a brightly colored red and yellow Indian textile ribbon.

"I'd let him play my pipes any day," said Angel. Transfixed, she watched the native Peruvian and his magical mouth.

"I'm having a smoke and a drink," declared Raven. She dashed to a nearby outdoor café, plopped down at an empty table, and lit up.

The others soon joined her on the Spanish, villa-style patio that overlooked the historic Market Square. Waist-high black iron railing separated them from the sightseeing tourists. Strolling Mariachi musicians sang and strummed on their box guitars. A sweet young Mexican waitress brought authentic chips and salsa. They ordered four large frozen margaritas and a refill for Raven. They sat comfortably in cushioned wooden barrel chairs around a circular wrought-iron table. Sipping their drinks and munching on chips, they had an opportunity to talk privately.

Raven exhaled a cloud of smoke aimed at the sky and sighed, "You know, we should be enjoying a late afternoon of sightseeing." Sarcastically, she added, "But . . . Noooo . . . , we're stuck in a cesspool! Bloodsucking parasites and an old fortune-telling gypsy are controlling our vacation!" Raven took a final drag and smashed the butt in the ashtray. "Let's get down to business. Dominic, tell us again what that old crone said. This time, leave out all the dramatics. Just cut to the chase!"

Uncomfortably, Dominic blurted, "Mona is going to join the ranks of the undead if we don't do something!" Dominic looked around the table and added, "The gypsy's last words were '*El Mercado*, silver bullets, and Charlie.'"

Exasperated, her voice short, Raven fixed Dominic with a stare and demanded, "What the hell does it mean?"

"Simple," explained Dominic. "We need silver bullets to kill the vampires."

"You mean silver bullets like the ones used by the Lone Ranger to keep law and order in the 'Old West' have the power to terminate a vampire?" asked Angel, eyebrows arched in amazement. "I thought they were for werewolves!"

"Wait a minute, whatever happened to just staking them?" Jaylyn asked, perplexed. "Why didn't you give us this information before we started playing this ridiculous game?"

Dominic closed her eyes briefly, her mind whirling. *Why do you expect me to have all the answers?* She wanted to snap back, but instead she admitted wearily, "I won't lie. I don't have all the answers, but I do know a vampire can be killed if shot through the heart with a silver bullet blessed by a priest. It stands to reason; we will have to get up close and friendly with vampires to kill them with stakes. If we don't catch them asleep in their coffins, where they're essentially helpless during their death sleep, they could get us before we have time to impale them. With a gun, we have a better chance of destroying the bastards and sending them back to pits of hellfire before they can nab us, rip out our throats, and suck us dry!"

Raven challenged. "Where are we going to get a gun? You know, the Brady Act requires a background check before you can purchase a firearm. I don't think any of us would hold up under the scrutiny of the FBI right now."

A moment of silence passed; Dominic unzipped her purse and sat it on the table. "Have a look." Inside, a silver-barreled handgun could be seen.

Bug-eyed, Koleen asked, "Where in the hell did you get a gun?"

"It's a .38 Smith & Wesson Special, and it doesn't matter where I got it. What's important is I have it, and I know how to use it." Dominic assured Koleen and added, "Now, all we need are the silver bullets."

Angel leaned close to Jaylyn and lowered her voice, "Wasn't her husband killed with a .38 Special?"

"Yeah. Funny, the murder weapon was never found."

"There it is! There's *El Mercado!*" Raven excitedly pointed to a large white building at the end of the square. "Slam your drinks ladies! Let's find Charlie." Hurriedly, the others gulped and followed her lead.

El Mercado was a typical market—a maze of shops that portrayed the interior of Mexico. Travelers could purchase a variety of imports including wrought iron, pottery, wood carvings, leather, and straw goods. Many stalls featured farm-fresh produce. "We're here to get silver bullets, NO SHOPPING," Dominic warned. "Got it?" Not waiting for their answer, she scooted past various shops filled with piñatas, Mexican dresses, curios, and candies. Heeding her words, they stuck together, tagging along.

Within a few minutes, Dominic discovered CHARLIE'S HACIENDA OF SILVER. The small jewelry stall housed a young lean Mexican man. As they entered, a wave of urgency swept over his face. "I've been expecting you."

The Watcher's body began to prepare for nightfall. Like a mortal emerging from deep sleep, he gradually surfaced. As the day said goodbye to night, he returned to the world of the living ready to take care of business.

Chapter 20

Hunger gnawed at the Watcher's gut. Reaching for a bottle of blood from the minibar refrigerator, he chugged, savoring the slightly bitter iron taste. "Breakfast of Champions," he chuckled. Tossing the empty in the trash, he dialed the Council. The women were armed and dangerous. They had acquired silver bullets from the Mexican black market.

In the inky darkness, Mona edged forward blindly. She ran her hands across the rough cement wall, searching for a way out of the sunless dungeon-like prison. The horny demon was pure evil. Laughingly admitting, he thought nothing of depriving her of her life and worse her salvation.

Escape . . . she had to escape.

Upon waking, she found Sven missing. Unable to locate her clothes, Mona braved the chill outside the coffin and fled. She didn't believe him when he had told her that vampires were really good guys who had just gotten bad press over the centuries. It was obvious; he was only softening her up for the kill! He would hold her as his personal sex slave and blood bank for days or maybe even weeks. A small slice of moonlight penetrated a crack in the boarded-up window; it toyed with the dust in the air. At sunrise, he would be returning to his secret, hiding place.

Hurry . . . she must hurry. Fearing the consequence of an attempted escape drove her. It wasn't wise to rile this vampire; she knew from her experience that he was high-strung and unpredictable. If he discovered that his dinner had up and flown the coop, it could be the straw that broke the camel's back.

Light-headed, she stumbled around the wall. Swallowing, she licked her dry lips nervously as she forced her legs to move. One step . . . two steps . . . *Where in the hell was the door?*

Feeling a sting, she gingerly touched the tender spot on her neck. *Damnation!* That bloodthirsty parasite had bitten her! He had been after her blood all along. Sex had only been a distraction. She had become his personal smorgasbord. The villainous fiend was leisurely draining her, taking a small amount each time to keep her alive longer.

He had tried to explain away his nature. "Vampires get hungry just like humans. Unfortunately for us, our next meal isn't as accessible. A drive-through isn't an option for a vampire."

Using his smooth, passionate charisma, he had tried to persuade her to join him as one of the children of the night. "Sleep all day, party all night, never grow old, and never die." It was a convincing argument until she woke up to the reality of her situation. To become one of them was to be lost for all eternity.

Mona put one foot in front of the other, sliding her way along the dusty floor.

Freezing in her tracks, she strained to hear. *Was it him?* She heard something. *Where in the hell was that sneaky vampire?* He was a killer, cold and calculating. A silver-tongued devil pleading for her understanding, "I'm not any different than you; I simply do what I have to in order to stay alive." Mona found little comfort in his explanation considering she was on his menu.

Behind her, she sensed him moving. Unhurried and methodical, he approached . . . closer and closer. Playing with her like a feral cat with a mouse, he enjoyed the hunt and anticipated the thrill of the kill.

Naked . . . No way to defend herself . . . Nowhere to hide . . . No way out . . . Trapped . . . DEAD! Panic tore through her. *Stay calm*, she warned.

Forcing herself to take deep, controlled breaths, she contemplated, *Didn't he understand the meaning of a one-night stand? Meet, have drinks, a few laughs, screw like rabbits, and then move on.* She had been attracted to him because he was the ultimate bad boy, and she had thought that maybe—just maybe—he was redeemable. *HUGE mistake! Vicious, wild animals don't make good house pets. No, a majority turned on their masters and ate them.*

Above her hammering heart, she heard the menacing footsteps of the murderous monster. The hunter was closing in on his prey. She cowered, waiting for her demise. There was only one thing to do. Pray that her friends weren't too late with the stakes and hammers.

At the touch of his cold finger on her cheek, she drew a sharp breath and let out, "Just get it over with! Don't make me suffer any longer."

The demonic creature breathed against her cheek. "Ahhhh, Mona, you can run, but you can't hide. We are forever linked. You're like a drug . . . a sweet addiction." Sven trapped Mona's arms to her sides. Glowing red eyes signaled his lustful craving. Scooping her up, his long strides melted into the darkness. Her struggles were useless; her screams, unanswered.

The Watcher read the text message and then set out for the River Walk. Good news! The persuasive techniques used by the interrogation unit of the Special Opts force had the blond vamp from the bar fight singing like a canary. The outlaws were hiding somewhere on this two-mile stretch of man-made cement river, and he would find them.

The information also came with a warning. The leader, Sven De La Boucher, was on the Council's top-ten-most-wanted list. He was known as a "Bad Ass." One of the slickest vampire mass murderers, he had killed nightly for centuries, undetected by mortals.

Chapter 21

The Watcher concealed himself in the darkness of Hotel Valencia's Mediterranean architecture as the light appeared in the hotel room.

"What the h . . ." Koleen flipped the light switch on, exposing a ransacked room.

"Stand back," warned Dominic as she withdrew her loaded pistol. "Is anybody in here? The "Judge" would like to meet you!" No answer. Dominic cocked the gun and cautiously entered. Maneuvering the obstacle course of upended chairs, scattered cushions, and overturned lamps, she made her way to the side of Koleen's slightly open bedroom door. Simultaneously, she hit the light and landed a powerful kick that nearly ripped the door off its hinges as it banged against the wall. "Clear!" Like a veteran detective, she swept the rest of the suite. "It's okay guys; come check it out!"

Silky lingerie and toiletries littered the floor. Travel bags had been turned inside out and their contents scattered about.

Furious, Koleen waded through the clutter to her bedroom. Abruptly, she bent and picked up her silk Italian camisole crumpled on the floor at her feet. "They weren't happy with just pilfering though our luggage; they had to trample all over our clothes with their filthy shoes."

"Whoever it was probably sniffed our underwear too!" fumed Raven as she used Dominic's black thong like a slingshot and launched it at her.

Angel rummaged through the tangled mess, picking up her possessions. The break-in had left her feeling exposed and vulnerable. Unable to make any sense of it, she asked, "Why would anyone break into our room?"

"Duh! Vampire Bible!" shrugged Jaylyn.

Dropping the camisole, Koleen frantically scrambled through what was left in her leather bag. She let out a blood-curdling scream. "Those dirty, rotten bottom-feeders stole it!"

Fire shot from her eyes. "That's it! Stomping back to the sitting room, she faced the others. "We didn't take bullshit like this from our husbands, and we're definitely not taking it from anyone else!" Koleen's clenched fist hammered her palm.

"Yeah, they're messing with the wrong bitches!" piped in Jaylyn, throwing the last of the retrieved items on her bed.

Angel rounded up the pill bottles strewn on her side of the room. Packing them back in her black satchel, she said, "Well, one thing's for certain, they weren't looking for drugs."

"Group meeting," Koleen declared. "Pull up a chair. Dominic, bring some paper and something to write with!" Dazed, but obeying Koleen's demands, they righted the chairs and joined her around the glass-topped table.

Koleen yanked the pen and pad from Dominic. "Let's figure out what's going on, who's responsible, and plan our attack. Got any ideas?"

Dominic proceeded to give her theory. "Anyone we've had contact with is a possible suspect. Our movements could have been easily monitored."

Raven stopped fidgeting in her chair and surprised the others with a confession, "I've been on edge the entire trip. I got spooked at the airport. I'm certain we were being watched then. A silver SUV with tinted windows and the black Hummer full of pretty-boy vampires tailed us to Texas. I was afraid to say anything because I thought I was letting my imagination get the best of me."

"I believe I danced with the guy responsible for all this. I'm sure he was at the airport and probably even the estate sale when I bought the Bible. I've got him pegged as the driver of the SUV too. It all adds up!" admitted Koleen, throwing her hands in the air.

"I still don't understand how one old, moldy book could get us into this bizarre mess. Stalked, kidnapped, and robbed. It's like we're stuck in some dreadful made-for-primetime-TV horror movie," Jaylyn professed.

"Well . . . ," Dominic paused and then added, "What about Derek Eastman? Whoever holds the Bible possesses the key to command all the evil powers of the dark side. Everyone connected to the paranormal wants it, and obviously, that sneaky slime ball knows we have it. He just doesn't want to pay for it!"

"Hey, the fortune-teller has fallen on hard times and probably sees the book as her chance to propel herself to the top of the psychic ladder of fame. Maybe she took it," offered Angel.

Koleen scribbled, "The bloodsuckers holding Mona could be plotting to take revenge on mortals for the centuries of persecution."

"The way I see it, find where Mona is being held captive, and we'll find your book, Koleen," asserted Raven. Moving back from the table, she suggested, "Let's do a little detective work. How 'bout taking one of those boat cruises tonight?"

"Sure. I'm ready to do a little hunting," Dominic smiled and patted her revolver.

The unexpected shrill ring of the hotel phone sent an electrifying jolt through them. Koleen jumped to answer it. Staring at the floor, she concentrated on what the caller had to say. After a moment, she gazed up at the women. Recognizing the voice on the other end, she said, "You may have the Bible, but you can't open it without the key. Fingering one of the gold chains dangling around her neck, she said with a smirk, "And, I have the key."

The Watcher caught the overpowering scent of decay laced with the night air; the rogue vampires were close. His senses also detected something else prowling the River Walk . . . the old gypsy witch!

Chapter 22

Scouring the River Walk, the Watcher finally discovered the rogues' lair. It wasn't long before three of the vampires slithered into the night. That left Sven alone with the woman; he was keeping the woman alive. Why? His efforts to locate the Bible must be failing. No doubt, he was pumping her for information. This could not go on indefinitely. Most mortals could only endure a few days of bloodletting before succumbing to death. Her days were numbered.

Sven lay on his side, watching Mona sleep. Absently he traced the tattoo. *Interesting . . .* Rising up on one arm, he brushed the curly tangle of hair away from the damp, pale skin of her neck and licked the bite. The flavor rolled around on his tongue like a sampling of good wine. Delicious, honey-sweet, full-bodied (the consistency of milk) with a hint of earthiness, the remnant lingered on his palette.

He had never seen anything so enticing, Mona naked and asleep. Sven couldn't resist whispering her name, "Mona."

After centuries of seducing women and gorging on every pleasure of the flesh imaginable, the hunt and conquest had lost its thrill; it had become too predictable. Bored, he had begun to consider women and even sex a bother and not worth his time or energy. Then . . . Mona came along. She could close her mind to him, keep her thoughts veiled, and guard her secrets. *Intriguing* . . .

The search for the ancient book had taken him across the centuries and around the world. His inside Council contact had led him to the women and Mona. He had intended to hold her as ransom for the Bible, but as fate would have it, he did not want to give her up. Not yet anyway. Was it lust, or was this the beginning of something more? Whatever he was feeling, one thing was certain—Mona was a rarity among mortal women, and he would be crazy to let her go.

Mona shifted against him, sending his groin into throbbing hardness. He sucked the scent of her down his nostrils and wrapped his arm around her lush, smooth ass. His erection pressed firmly at her yielding flesh slipping snuggly between her legs. Sven leaned in and whispered her name again.

A sensual moan escaped Mona's lips. "Am I a vampire now?"

Amused, he pulled her closer. He teased the two puncture marks with his tongue before answering. "It takes more than the 'Vampire Kiss' to make you one of us. In order to become a vampire, you would need to drink from my body as I did from yours. If that doesn't happen, you will become weaker and weaker as I feed upon you . . . until finally . . . you waste away, welcoming death. And, that would really be a shame," he said sincerely.

"Wait a minute . . . are you telling me I only have two choices? I have to become a vampire sex slave or die?"

"Consider yourself lucky that I'm even giving you a choice. Most of my victims aren't so fortunate."

Curiosity getting the best of her, she dared to ask, "How did you become a vampire then?"

"I was given a choice, the same as you. It happened a long time ago, in another century, in another land. As a young French nobleman, I took part in the Fourth Crusades in 1202. I went to the Holy Land looking for adventure and came back with a consuming hunger. I had become a vampire. I have lived on the dark side for more than eight hundred years."

Mona thought, *This is insane. I'm being held captive, in a coffin, by an eight hundred-year-old bloodsucking sex fiend.* Panic gripped her, and she screamed a psychic SOS to her friends. *HELP ME!* Dominic's words from the vampire bar flashed through her mind, calming her frayed nerves. "Show no fear." Still having trouble wrapping her mind around the implications of his answer but composed, she pulled back from him. Choosing her words carefully, she said, "That explains a lot of things including your experience with . . . sex . . . women."

Taking her halting explanation as a compliment, Sven smiled. He knew from the quickening beat of her heart, she was remembering how he could leave her wet and begging for his touch.

Leaning in, enjoying her discomfort, he continued, "I was part of the military expedition of knights that seized the great city of Constantinople.

Out of control, the crusading army ruthlessly sacked Constantinople. The soldiers destroyed, defiled, or stole everything they could get their hands on. Many valuable religious artifacts were part of the loot including an ancient scroll belonging to a cult of vampires.

"During the siege, many of the Crusaders fell ill. It was rumored that we had been cursed for the horrible atrocities committed. Day by day, the infected men grew weaker until they finally died. As it turned out, it wasn't an illness or even a curse killing the soldiers but a nest of vampires using the war as a cover to recruit for their dark army. The most skilled of the knights were allowed to make the choice. I chose to become a vampire warrior. My orders: retrieve the stolen scroll that had been secreted out of the city along with other valuable relics when the Crusaders returned home. Once in Europe, many relics not confiscated by the Church were hidden and forgotten.

After centuries of failure and frustration tracking down false leads, a few of the more ambitious vampires, like me, grew tired of following orders. Branded rogues, we continued the search on our own. Whoever holds the Bible holds the fate of both living and dead. Your friend has it. I have been looking for this book for a long, long time, Mona, and I mean to have it."

Sven tenderly touched the corner of her mouth with one finger and then traced a lazy path to the bite on her neck. The hunger threatened to consume him. "There is no turning back now, Mona. I will not allow you to leave me. You and the Bible are mine, and I intend to keep you both for all eternity." Aggressively, he placed his mouth on Mona's; his tongue dueled with hers.

Eternity! Round two. Instant slut took on a whole new meaning. Sven mounted her; his throbbing erection probed her wetness, seeking entrance. Her legs opened, allowing the massive intrusion. Her silky warmth contracted, turning Sven into a power driver. Each thrust intensified, coming faster, harder, and deeper. Mona's pain was now pleasure. Arching closer, she felt a sharp pinch at her throat and shuttered. A raging fire burned inside her as he fed on her precious blood.

The Watcher knew that it was only a matter of time before he faced the ancient warrior, Sven.

Chapter 23

The Watcher's gaze escorted the river cruiser as it wound through the canal. Night was a dangerous time for the women, but their safety was assured as long as they stayed in the boat.

The river cruiser traversed the narrow canal under a spectacular display of twinkling lights that reflected off the water. Dozens of riverside cafes, bistros, and elegant restaurants lined the River Walk. Colorful umbrellas adorned the outdoor patios that stretched to the river's edge.

Rich history of the San Antonio River was narrated through the captain's headset microphone. Raven was not entertained. Her acute sixth sense caught something unworldly lurking just out of sight. *Oh, my God, this was scary!* Dark, fleeting shapes appeared again and again, haunting the landscape. They vaporized, reappearing at the next bridge, lamppost, or bend in the river. *It had to be those sneaky yellow-bellied vampires. Nothing else could move that fast.*

"Something wrong?" Koleen asked, noticing Raven's distress. "You look kind of pale."

Scowling into the darkness, she whispered, "Vampires are hiding everywhere!"

Hearing Raven, Dominic confided, "That's not all. I think, I just saw that gypsy woman eyeing us from the last pedestrian overpass."

"Ladies and gentlemen, around the next bend, on your left, you will see an old, abandoned hotel." Heads swiveled as the captain continued, "Soon, it will be replaced by a seventy-two-million-dollar glass-and-chrome paranormal museum. San Antonio's finest philanthropist, Derek Eastman, is the brainchild behind this project."

"That's the backstabber that has my Bible," snapped Koleen. "What do you think of your long-legged Texan now, Dominic?"

"Revenge is sweet. We'll deal with that raunchy urban cowboy later, and it won't take a silver bullet," Dominic assured Koleen. "Mona's our top priority at the moment; let's try another telepathic contact right here and now, ladies."

The five straightened, tuned-in to Mona's psychic hotline, and channeled their energy. The noise and lights of the River Walk journey blurred and faded. In unison, they whispered Mona's name.

Tourists, unnerved by the strange vibration shrouding the air around the women, slid down the red, leather bench, putting distance between them and the odd occurrence.

Rubbing her throbbing temples, Dominic said, "We've got to hurry. I'm getting an SOS from Mona." The others confirmed that Mona was indeed sending out a psychic distress signal.

Koleen added, "The glitter has worn off Mona's vampire romance; she's desperate and begging for our help!"

"Get a look at that hotel," gasped Angel as the captain throttled down and drifted, yielding the right-of-way to an impatient water taxi. "Why didn't we just go to Padre Island, lay in the sun, and drink frozen margaritas?"

Mona's prison sat frozen in time, illuminated by two small security lights at the base of the stone fortress. The hotel was a Dracula castle look-alike straight from Bram Stocker's novel. Round towers at each exterior corner of the massive keep loomed over the dozen semicircular sentry boxes guarding the entrance.

"It's like an old black-and-white horror flick." Jaylyn's voice quivered.

"Yeah, and it's probably crawling with vampires," said Angel. She squinted in hope of getting a better look. "They could be watching us right now!"

"Stop it. You're going to scare yourselves silly with that kind of talk," warned Raven. "Mona is our friend. We can't let fear get in our way."

Dominic took charge before the argument escalated. "Now that we know Mona's location, we can formulate a plan to get her out without getting killed in the process."

Floating passed the crumbling stone monstrosity, Jaylyn jumped up, causing the boat to pitch violently. "Hey, there's a real estate sign!"

Tourists screamed. The captain bellowed, "Sit down, lady!"

Ignoring the pissed-off looks and admonishment of the captain, Angel patted the seat for Jaylyn to sit back down.

"Yeah, and it doesn't have that little red sign plastered across the front announcing that it's sold," added Dominic, straining to get the broker's name.

"That can only mean one thing. Good old Derek hasn't closed the deal yet. If we can convince the broker we're interested in the site, we might get a tour tomorrow. Once inside, we can snoop and hopefully uncover the vampire hideout and Mona's love nest," said Koleen. She was confident in their ability to pull it off. "One way or another, we're getting in!"

He was divided—obey the code or help the humans. If he was true to the vampire code of laws, he would stay focused and carry out his mission. But—and he hated it when there was a "but" involved—what was he going to do about the women?

Chapter 24

The Watcher paced the length of the castle tower. Persistence had prevailed; now, the troublemakers were literally at death's door. As he expected, he would have to protect them. Protection would cost them the Vampire Bible.

Pulling off Commerce Street into the underground garage, the real estate agent popped a breath mint. "Damn, late again!" Earl Reman said as he glanced at his watch. The Eastman deal was at best lukewarm. The arrogant millionaire's offer was way below asking price. Earl hated negotiating with the tightwad, but despite all the quibbling, Reman had stood firm on the price.

How else was a man to get ahead? Ms. O'Brien's call was the opportunity to do just that. If he made a good impression, he could unload the property and proudly announce to Mr. Eastman that the estate had been sold. Dealing with members of the opposite sex had netted him considerable profit in the past; he would again work his magic to dump this albatross.

They had agreed to meet at Clancy's Outdoor Pub near the garage. From there, they would walk the short distance to the property. Reman parked his ten-year-old ragtop caddie, grabbed his briefcase, opened the door, and slid out. Tucking in his maroon silk shirt and adjusting the gold chains adoring his neck, he scurried to the stairs leading down to the River Walk.

His clients were waiting, visibly impatient. Adjusting his polyester pants, he quickened his pace to greet them. Earl flashed them a dazzling smile that revealed his pointed rodent-like teeth.

The women were unimpressed with the agent's attempt to win them over. In fact, a sense of urgency was overtaking them. Not only was the sun sinking, the once clear Texas sky was filling with dark clouds. This, coupled with the heavy, oppressive air, was a sure sign of bad weather.

"Damn, that 'Over the Hill Romeo'!" How does he expect to sell anything! His late arrival has cost us precious time and put us in a risky position. It's now a race to beat the setting sun. We've got to get in and stake those vampires before the sun goes down," complained Koleen to Dominic as the cocky realtor approached.

"It'll be OK. Remember, we have a gun," Dominic reassured Koleen. Stifling the giggle that threatened to escape, Dominic thought, *This guy thinks he's a lady's man, but he looks more like an aging ferret.* Short, his pot belly jiggled and hung over a white belt that held up his pants. White scuffed loafers completed a picture of a middle-aged male experiencing an identity crisis. Who was he trying to fool with a comb-over and a fake-and-bake tan? He was definitely a throwback from the disco era.

Koleen had the honor of greeting the poor sap. "Mr. Reman," she said cordially.

"Earl, ma'am . . . just call me Earl. Sorry for the delay, but that San Antonio traffic can be quite a pain in the neck!" Earl's excuse fell on deaf ears.

"Thanks for agreeing to show the property on such short notice. As I said in our phone conversation earlier, my associates and I are looking for a place on the River Walk for our adult fantasy vacation retreat. Restoring the castle to its former glory would be the perfect setting for a venture like this," Koleen said with a naughty wink.

"We better get going. It looks like we might get wet. I didn't know it was supposed to rain today," complained Dominic.

Earl turned to Dominic and seized the opportunity to play weatherman. "Where have you been, babe? The eye of Hurricane Dolly came ashore on Padre Island this morning and is heading our way. It's all over the news."

"We've been busy wheeling and dealing this week. We haven't been paying attention to the news or forecasts," replied Koleen defensively.

"Well, the mother of all storms is bearing down on us!" he informed her.

Great, mumbled Koleen to herself. *It's not enough that we have to battle the supernatural; now, we have to contend with Mother Nature. It really couldn't get much worse, could it?*

Realtor Reman led them down the winding River Walk. In some places, the trees arched over their heads, forming a tunnel. Rising wind whistled and moaned as it funneled through the passageway. Branches bent and leaves lost their hold as nature unleashed its power. "How much further is it?" yelled Koleen, hearing a crash.

"We're here," he said as they scrambled across the bridge. Earl fumbled nervously in his pocket for keys, and then, after locating them, wrestled the lock open. Hurriedly, he shoved the gates wide and placed his briefcase on the inside concrete bench. "We might need these," he explained. Entering his case, he produced three cheap plastic flashlights. The round dot stickers advertised his garage sale bargains. Keeping one, he handed the other two to Dominic; she gave one to Jaylyn. She would share the other with Koleen.

Earl switched his on by beating it against his palm. "Let's have a look, shall we?"

"The sooner, the better," encouraged Dominic. Leading them with his flickering beam, they hustled down the shadowy pathway.

Jaylyn, Angel, and Raven had taken up position as the rear guards. Jaylyn swept the bushes along the trail with the flashlight. Armed with garlic, baby tears, and wooden stakes, they searched the grounds for any suspicious movement.

Leaning away from Angel, Jaylyn gagged, "Man, I think you went overboard on that garlic perfume. You smell like a garbage pail in an Italian restaurant!"

Pushing Jaylyn, Angel replied, "Hey, if you don't like it, don't stand so close. I'm not taking any chances. I don't want one of those bloodsuckers sneaking up on me and ripping my throat out."

"Well, you're safe! He's going to smell you long before he gets close enough to chew on your neck," Raven pointed out.

"Hey, ladies, how about grabbing a bite to eat after we look over the property? I'm treating. It's the least I can do since I kept you waiting." Poor Earl had missed lunch, and dining with this bunch looked like a lot of fun. "I know a great Italian restaurant near here."

Jaylyn jabbed Angel in the ribs with her elbow and burst out laughing. "See, what did I tell you? Little heavy on the garlic."

"That's a very nice offer, but we've already eaten," Koleen answered.

They came to a standstill in front of double doors; Earl placed an oversized key in the massive black iron padlock and gave it a twist. The monstrous doors swung back, and they darted in just as the rain set in.

Earl played his light around the debris-littered foyer. Icy fingers of fear inched up Dominic's spine. They could have stepped back in time. The gray stone walls were draped with heavy tapestries reminiscent of the medieval era. A coat of arms with two swords tilted unevenly on one wall. A rusty suit of armor was stationed on both sides of the spiraling stairway leading to the floors above.

Suddenly, the air exploded with a thunderous clap; streaks of lightning flashed through the window. At that moment, they noticed the statue-like figure at the bottom of the staircase moving. Everyone screamed . . . even Earl. Their flashlights revealed the broken-down conjuror, Madam Zorba.

"Hey, this is private property, not a homeless shelter. How in 'Sam Hill' did you get in here anyway?" Earl yelled in his best, manly voice.

"I know her; let me take care of this," Dominic intervened as Earl gladly stepped back with the rest of the women. Dominic moved to confront her. What she had to say was for the old woman's ears only. "What are you doing here?" insisted Dominic angrily.

The gypsy's claw-like hand latched onto Dominic and drew her closer. "I'm here for the Bible. Give it to me, and I will help you defeat the vampires."

"Get your hand off me! You've been a real big help, haven't you? While we were getting silver bullets, someone stole the Bible. Didn't you see THAT in your crystal ball?" jeered Dominic.

"Tell me who has it," she hissed through clenched teeth.

"Who are you to be making demands? Here's the way it's goin' down. I'm going to tell you, and then I don't ever want to see your wrinkled, prune face again. If you want it so badly, go see the Texas oilman, Derek Eastman." Dominic smiled. This would be the finest revenge for the double-crossing, long-legged cowboy.

Searching Dominic's face, the witch was satisfied that she had been told the truth. Her black skirt stirred up a whirlwind of leaves and debris from the floor as she swooped past them exiting the premises.

The women circled Dominic and questioned, "What's going on?"

"She wanted the book, of course, but don't worry," she replied. "I just took care of Eastman. As we all know, paybacks are a bitch!"

Motioning to Earl, Koleen said, "Come on, let's get goin'."

Earl led the way through the main floor, pointing out the unique features that made the property a great buy for the right investor. On heightened alert, they half—listened while discreetly poking around for clues.

Earl halted the tour at the last unopened door on the main floor. "This leads to the wine cellar, but I don't recommend going down there," Earl advised.

Dominic whispered to Koleen, "This has to be the vampire's lair."

Pushing him aside, Dominic ignored his nervous twitch and opened the door. She took charge guiding the faithful four down decrepit, rotting steps that creaked under their weight. Last in the descending line was Raven. As she passed the chicken-livered realtor, she snatched his flashlight. "Don't reckon you'll be needing this."

"Ladies . . . ladies . . . come back . . . please," he pleaded. Earl hovered at the top of the landing filling the doorway. "Those stairs are steep; come back tomorrow when there's more light," he beseeched in a high-pitched, squeaky voice.

The Watcher was with them; his presence veiled by darkness. His senses detected the rogues surfacing from their slumber. Ravenous upon wakening, they would set upon the foolish women and devour them.

Chapter 25

A night predator, the Watcher carried himself confidently through the darkness. His acute hearing and night vision, better than 20/20 in total darkness, guided his every move.

B lackness at the foot of the steps yawned ahead of the amateur vampire slayers like a bottomless pit. Swatting cobwebs and breathing moldy air, they safely reached the bottom. Huddled and mute, the assailants' flashlights explored the surroundings while their ears strained to detect any sounds of life or the dead. They spotted two hallways leading in opposite directions.

Dominic gave the orders. "We'll have to split up. Raven, Angel, Jaylyn, take the hallway to the left; Koleen and I will take the other. Remember, this is real. Vampires will kill you! Show no mercy. Be quick and stake the bloody butchers in their coffins."

"What are you doing?" Earl called anxiously from the top of the stairs. "I thought you were just going to have a quick look."

They pretended not to hear him. If he couldn't be bothered to accompany them, they were not interested in his ill-placed concern.

Dominic drew the loaded double-action.38 Special from her pocket. Gun in one hand, flashlight in the other, she bravely set out. Koleen, armed with stakes and hammer, followed her closely.

"Where's our gun?" Raven asked as she led Jaylyn and Angel.

"We're covered. We have learned that you can't leave your ass swingin' in the wind with those two. We have our own fire power," said Angel, holding it under the light for Raven to see. "Lucky for us, Jaylyn and I picked this up at the vampire conference."

They sent me to kill vampires with wooden stakes and two imbeciles. Upset at their sheer stupidity, Raven asked, "Is it a full moon? Have you two completely lost it? They'll slaughter us. Even Custer made a better last stand. What kind of damage do you expect to do with that ninety-eight cent squirt gun?"

"It's an old Indian trick. Don't be deceived; this little beauty is packing baby tears. We're loaded for vampire," boasted Jaylyn, not understanding Raven's sarcasm.

Having a change of heart and kicking at a long-tailed fur ball, she reluctantly inquired, "Does that stuff work on ankle-bitin' rodents?"

"Didn't you hear me the first time? We are loaded for vampires. Not bear, not rodents. VAMPIRES!" Angel firmly repeated.

Sorry she had asked, Raven hissed, "Shut up!" She turned hell-bent on completing the mission. Not far, the hall ended at a closed door.

Holding her breath, Raven turned the doorknob and thrust her shoulder into it. It didn't budge. Again, she pushed . . . Nothing.

"Give it a PULL!" Frustrated, Jaylyn ground out.

Smart-ass, Raven thought. Sure enough, the door's rusty hinges yielded with a cr . . . ea . . . k. Heart-pounding adrenaline surged through the would-be executioners as their beams fell on three separate coffins.

Passing the light to Angel, Raven whispered, "OK, it's curtain time. Let's finish them. Ready? On the count of three. One . . . two . . . three."

Jaylyn's trembling hand raised the lid of the first coffin. Angel trapped and targeted the vampire's breast in her light. Cautiously, Raven placed the stake, raised the hammer, and with a powerful downward slam, nailed the devil to his bed. As the stake pierced his heart, a fountain of blood spewed out, splattering the assassins. His eyes flew open, pinning them with hate and pain. Withering and thrashing about, his desperate hands clawed at the protruding dagger of death. Defeated, he gulped his last breath and went limp. Jaylyn slammed the lid.

"Man, what a rush!" declared Raven. "Hope the other two are this easy." Determined and confidences boosted, they moved to the next coffin to carry out the gruesome deed again. It was an exact repeat of the first.

Angel sung under her breath a line from an old rock 'n' roll classic, "Another One Bites the Dust."

Jaylyn joined in. "And another one's gone." The duet abruptly came to an end.

The death squad was drawn to the last coffin. They witnessed the lid easing open. Raven and Jaylyn prepared for the attack by holding up their crosses; Angel aimed her plastic pistol. Eyes blazing, the vampire lunged from his bed, landing in front of them. "Shoot the son-of-a-bitch!" screamed Raven.

The creature threw an arm across his eyes to thwart the power radiating from their weapons. He howled in pain as the baby tears seared his flesh. Wounded, he skirted the vampire slayers and bound through the door.

Horrifying, high-pitched screams and a tumbling struggle echoed down the stairs; it ended with a heavy thump. Koleen and Dominic cringed. Earl had become the latest casualty in the vampire war. "We're too late!" Dominic screamed, dropping the flashlight. Darkness engulfed them as the light hit the concrete floor. Panicked, she scrambled after it.

"Damn it, Dominic. We don't have time for this. If you can't handle the flashlight, give it to me," Koleen ranted. "How in the hell were you going to shoot the gun and hold a flashlight anyway?" Fumbling around on hands and knees, Dominic finally located the flashlight. She gave it a firm whack, and it flickered back to life. Snatching the light, Koleen took the lead. She walked to the end of the hall and opened the door. *Mona was alive!*

Vaporizing, his body faded into nothingness and disappeared. He moved silently down the hall and materialized as a swirling dark shadow in the room ahead of Koleen. The ancient rogue was waiting for him.

Chapter 26

The storm intensified, mirroring the Watcher's anticipation of battle. Torrential rains driven by the wind lashed the stone fortress. Zigzagged lightning streaks flashed through the splintered boards that had been haphazardly nailed to the cellar's windows.

Sven sized up the intruders. The Council had sent their best; he was a formidable opponent, a seasoned warrior like himself.

As for the meddling mortals, he had heard and smelled them before they entered. Their fear was laced with the thrill of the hunt. These creatures had obviously walked on the "dark side" before and relished the chance to experience that high again. These pitiful humans were no match for his strength. Sven laughed out loud at the stakes and hammer. *Did she really think she could get close enough to pull that trick?* If she tried, he'd rip her arms off!

However, the one holding the gun did pose a threat. If she did manage to land a shot, it would slow him down, turning the tide in favor of his challenger. He could survive any non-fatal injury including a bullet wound. Within seconds, he would be healed and still have a chance to demolish his opponent. He decided to take care of the Council's man first; he really believed that the women's objective was to rescue Mona.

As the vampires rose off the floor, they circled in the air arena, formulating their line of attack. Dropping stakes and hammer, Koleen rushed to aid Mona. Dominic backed her up. Koleen grabbed Mona's crumpled clothes and instructed her to put them on.

"Keep them in your beam," Dominic ordered, aiming the .38 with both hands. "These demons ruined our vacation; they deserve to die again!" The dark power, strong and angry, grew within her.

Hisses erupted from their wide-open mouths, exposing vicious, glistening fangs. The Watcher savagely planted the first blow as they sprang toward each other. The powerful right split Sven's lip and sent his head back. Flaming red eyes stabbed his rival. He spit out blood and charged like a spinning tornado. Sven's assault was evenly matched; the two exchanged devastating blows and kicks.

Dominic and Koleen found it impossible to track and accurately pinpoint the dueling duo. Chasing every hit had left them dizzy; they waited listening for an end. Sven's strike slammed the Watcher into the unyielding wall. Unconscious, he met the concrete with a nosedive.

Sven staggered, knowing the Enforcer wouldn't be down long. He angled for the discarded stake. Seething with rage, he lunged for it and advanced on the disabled warrior. Sven firmly seized the killing stick with both hands and raised it over his head.

"NO!" Mona screamed as she threw herself at Dominic. The gun exploded. Sven collapsed. With a howl, he raged, "Silver bullets!"

Mona rushed to her captor's side. She was torn; her entire life had been a flirtation with danger. Mona had walked on the wild side more than once and had been faced with disastrous consequences each time. The lure of the forbidden and dangerous was intoxicating. Now, she was involved with the ultimate "Bad Boy," a killing machine.

What had transpired in this dark room would take time to sort out. She had discovered the many facets of her sexuality and shattered all taboos. Together, they had explored the pleasure pain of sharp fangs and bloodletting. In her mind, there was no turning back the clock to what polite society called "normal sex."

Who was she to judge Sven for his crimes against the living anyway? He wasn't the only one haunted by dark deeds from the past. She knew evil lurked in the heart of man just waiting for a chance to rear its ugly head. She had answered the call of evil; her husband had paid the price.

Despite her feelings, Mona knew she didn't want him to die. Sven sensed Mona's uncertainty; her mind was no longer shielded. He opened his eyes to comfort her. "Mona, you saved me. If that bullet had found its mark, It would have meant a slow painful death. Your friend is very clever. Silver bullets are to vampires what kryptonite is to the comic book hero, Superman. A deadly poison . . . ," Sven whispered, his voice strained from the excruciating pain produced by the silver.

"Damn! I can't believe you missed! I thought you were a crack shot?" Koleen taunted Dominic.

"Hey, I was ambushed by Mona. You were supposed to keep her occupied. Remember, I'm still armed and dangerous. So don't push your luck," Dominic returned.

Coming around, the Watcher sprung to his feet and assessed the situation. The Ancient One was down, but he was still potentially dangerous. Grabbing the stake, he knelt and placed it over the wounded vampire's heart.

"Stop!" Mona screamed. "Koleen, do something! Give him that damn Bible! That's what this is all about anyway."

"Please, wait!" Koleen yelled.

Dominic set her sights on the kneeling man just as Jaylyn, Angel, and Raven barged in, adding to the turmoil. Ready to offer assistance, Raven flashed her light around and chuckled. "Well, looks like we have a 'Mexican standoff'—on our hands."

"Maybe we can come to some sort of compromise. Put down the gun, give me the Bible, and I will let your friend's lover live."

"Well, there's just one little problem with that scenario. The Bible was stolen. However, there is some good news; it can't be opened without this," Koleen said sarcastically, holding up the key. As much as it galled her to give up her ticket to easy street, Koleen relented, "I will trade you the key and the name of the thief for the life of the vampire."

The Watcher weighed his options and offered, "I will not kill him, but I can't set him free. He has violated the Vampire Code and must stand trial for his transgressions. It's my sworn duty to destroy him if he tries to escape."

Stroking Mona's arm, Sven sighed, "Looks like I'm between a rock and a hard place. He paused before continuing, as if contemplating the ramifications of his next words. "Synthetic blood doesn't sound so bad when faced with the alternative." Melting with Mona's mind only, he shared, "Besides, my inside Councilman will spare my life, and soon, I will return to you, my luscious pet."

"If you do come back, I hope your feeding addiction has been cured. If it's as awful as my chocolate donut addiction, you may be gone for some time," transmitted Mona, smiling and patting her middle.

Keeping an eye on Sven, the Watcher stepped to Koleen and extended his hand, "The key."

Removing the key from her neck, she placed it in his waiting hand.

The Watcher captured Koleen's hand in both of his and deliberately brought them to his lips. Black eyes meeting green, he whispered, "To know a vampire's name comes with special privileges. When given freely to a mortal, it's a pledge of protection. My name is Keegan. All you have to do is speak it, and I will be come to you."

This was getting out of control. She was not ready for that level of commitment especially to a . . . man who had been dead for centuries. "Thanks, but no thanks," she replied and pulled free from his cold touch.

Dejected, Keegan moved to Sven and knelt down. Their images began to break apart like tiny specks in a dust storm, and within seconds, they had vanished.

The secrets of the vampire world were safe. Without the key, the Bible was useless. The Ancient One would be turned over to the Council. He would be given a choice: change his eating habits or be annihilated. All the loose ends tied up neatly. Just the way he liked it. As for the redhead, time would tell.

Epilogue

Night welcomed the Watcher. He strode to his favorite vantage point. A final glimpse of Koleen, and then duty called . . . a new mission . . . different dangers . . . but the same old gut-wrenching loneliness.

Two of the women sat on the balcony of the fashionable Hotel Valencia. Thousands of lights formed a magical canopy over the San Antonio River Walk. Each silently surveyed the parade of river gondolas that passed below. Leisurely sipping on what had become their favorite drink, the Vampire Kiss martini, they sat for a time captivated by the old-world charm of the city and the allure of its darker side. Finally, Mona turned to Dominic and said," I thought the trip went quite well, all things considered."

A slight twitch tugged at the corners of Mona's mouth. As their eyes met and locked over the patio table, the laughter began. It started as soft chuckles and instantly advanced into uncontrollable waves of something more sinister as the other members of the Black Widow Society spilled out onto the balcony. The ornate gold crucifixes dangling from their necks glimmered in the last rays of sunlight. The six women began recanting what they believed to be the most memorable events of the past week. But in the end, they all had to agree, it began somewhat ominously with the discovery of the Vampire Bible.

"I propose a toast to Koleen." The women saluted Koleen with a clink of their glasses. "Thanks for the memories," said Mona in earnest.

"Yeah, it will be hard to forget being stalked by a pack of ruthless vampires," said Jaylyn.

"I'll never forget the look on Koleen's face when she stumbled from the bathroom half-naked after being felt up by a dead man," mused Angel as everyone chuckled.

"What about Dominic's psycho Texan breaking into our room, sniffing our underwear on the pretext of stealing that moldy old book?" asked Raven.

Scratching her head, Jaylyn said, "I'll never understand how that shabby, unkempt gypsy thought we'd give up the Bible."

Dejected and a little put out, Dominic said, "Looks like Mona was the only lucky one this trip. She got all the good sex while we wore ourselves out running all over San Antonio trying to rescue her."

Provoked by Dominic's comment, Mona replied, "He said he'd be back for seconds after his stint in vampire rehab is up." Cupping her breasts and giving them a lift, she smirked, "He didn't get enough of THIS the first go-around."

"What about Koleen's mystery man? I wager there's more to that than meets the eye," Angel said, giving Koleen a knowing wink.

Laying everyone's scorecard on the table, Dominic announced, "It's official. I have tallied up everyone's score, and I declare Mona the winner of the game." This threw the women into a frenzy of denial.

"How do you figure that?" demanded Koleen. "I was ravaged by a walking corpse in a nasty bar bathroom. You know, it's even dangerous to use the crapper in one of those places."

"Oh, brother, are you a few fries short of a Happy Meal?" Raven accused. "Jaylyn, Angel, and I rubbed out two of Dracula's offspring!"

"We would have had a third, but my water cannon gave out!" Angel said sadly.

"It was a cheapo . . . inferior plastic, I expect," consoled Jaylyn, reaching over and patting Angel on the arm.

"I agree, you guys acted with uncommon valor, but Mona is a survivor of a vicious vampire attack. Held captive for days, she was nearly turned into one of the undead. I declare Mona the undisputable winner and pass the torch to her." Turning to Mona, Dominic said sincerely, "Good luck planning our next reality game. I'm here for you if you need me."

"No, no, please . . . DON'T ask for her advice on anything to do with our next vacation. Look what a mess she made of this trip," they all chimed in.

From the shadows, he wondered how soon it would be before Koleen spoke his name. Reluctantly, he turned and melted into the night.

Black Widow Fantasy

Six Black Widow Sisters—tried and true
Left for vacation as they usually do
Heading west to Texas this time
To relax and drink margaritas with lime
Dominic chose the fantasy game they would play
Tallying their scorecards each and every day
"Vampire slayers we'll be
Arm yourselves with these!"
Garlic, gold crosses, baby tears, and stakes
"Use them wisely—make no mistakes!"
Mona laughed and smiled
You're one crazy bitch! I'm game. Let's get wild!
Everyone played along
Not knowing that things would go terribly wrong
For don't you see?
Vampires were a reality
Koleen, the Red—had acquired the book of the undead
Vampires weren't happy, they wanted their necks instead
Stalked by the creatures day and night
They were clueless of their plight
Raven, the Indian beauty
Drove the rental van, that was her duty
Angel carried drugs in her little black satchel
She offered them freely, she wasn't bashful
Drinking, dancing, flirting, fighting and fun
Til Mona was kidnapped by the Ancient One
Bloodthirsty beasts
Ready to feast

Saving herself, she spread her legs

"Take me, Baby" she begs

Rescue their friend, they must

So in an old gypsy, they put their trust

Betrayed they made their own way to the vampire's lair

While the warriors from the dark side were already there

Black Widow Spiders on a mission to kill

Ready to pounce and enjoy the thrill

In the end, one final trade

His life for the book and VAMPIRE REHAB was made

Jaylyn, quiet as can be

Wrote it all down for you and me